UNRAVELING DARKNESS

SCOUT BOOK 2

ALEX LIDELL

DANGER BEARING PRESS

ALSO BY ALEX LIDELL

Young Adult Fantasy Novels

TIDES

FIRST COMMAND (Prequel Novella)

AIR AND ASH

WAR AND WIND

SEA AND SAND

SCOUT

TRACING SHADOWS

UNRAVELING DARKNESS

TILDOR

THE CADET OF TILDOR

New Adult Fantasy Romance

POWER OF FIVE (Reverse Harem Fantasy)

POWER OF FIVE

MISTAKE OF MAGIC

SIGN UP FOR NEW RELEASE NOTIFICATIONS

at www.subscribepage.com/TIDES

Reviews are an author's lifeblood. Please consider saying a few words about this book on Amazon.

KALI

*T*he king is dead and I'm pulling his son into the woods before his head joins his father's on the palace's flagpole.

My mind is numb. Screams and the clashing of blades echo in the air, which is thick with the copper stench of blood. The palace courtyard before us is a killing field, with Bishop Bahir's red-clad holy guards butchering the royal court.

Minutes ago, Prince William, Luca, Trace, and I were all in Questioner Calvin's dungeon, where a pair of young girls had implicated Trace in smuggling whisperers to Everett. A serious accusation that threatened to lead to accurate questions about Trace's loyalties. Minutes ago, I was fearing for Trace's life. And then, within the time it takes to slice a sword through flesh, none of that mattered any longer.

Prince Wil of Dansil pulls back against my grip. "Wait."

"King Firehorn is *dead*," I tell him again, my heart pounding. The sooner I can get Wil to safety, the sooner I can return for my sister, Leaf, who's still caught in the besieged palace. "It's a coup. Bishop Bahir is taking the palace by force, and you need to move."

Wil twists about, blood draining from his face as he sees the bloody head I wanted to protect him from. "Father."

"We've no time for this." Trace grabs the back of the prince's tunic and drags him around to the back of the palace, toward the North Wood that's to be our refuge. Considering who Trace truly is—the long-believed-dead Prince Rune of Everett, masquerading as a guardsman of the Dansil king—Trace's commitment to protecting Wil even now is . . . interesting.

Everett and Dansil are at war over Sylthia, a piece of land that Everett captured two dozen years ago, but this attack is not Everett's doing at all. While Dansil was focused on Everett, Bishop Bahir and his Order of the Goddess following have been infiltrating the Dansil court. Seizing power. Allying with the Viva Sylthia terror mongers to get us to this day.

Luca, Calvin, and the girls—Alexa and Jasmine—are at the North Wood already, moving in deeper when they see us coming. We make an odd crew, but there is no time to choose company when a coup strikes. Cold wind and sunlight whip our faces, beech and ash branches reaching out to snag our clothing.

Pushing my way to the head of the group, I take the lead to guide them on the path of best concealment. A trained scout, I've spent enough time here in the persona of Kal, a male guard trainee, to know the woods inside and out.

"In there," I say, pointing to a tight cluster of trees where long-needled firs droop their branches low and thick.

The group obeys, and a few heartbeats later, we enter the small, covered clearing. Calvin and the girls are breathing hard, the older man bracing his hand against a tree trunk for balance. Good enough. Turning away from them, I creep back toward the thick branches, pushing the needles aside carefully to survey my return path. I'll have to move quickly if I'm to make it to Leaf in time.

"You can't go back now, Kal, if that's what you are contemplating," Trace says behind me. "Not for anyone."

Trace's sister, Raza, is still in the palace, I realize. Wil's sister, Violet, too—she's somewhere in Delta. I'm not the only one with a beloved sibling still inside the slaughter.

But I will be the one going back. The others can make their own choices. "Let them catch their breath, then keep going," I murmur over my shoulder. "I'll catch up."

Trace's iron grip clamps on to my shoulder. "I said *no*. It's suicide."

I twist toward him with a snarl. "I wasn't asking you, Trace. Let. Go."

He doesn't. Blood rushes to my face, my muscles pulsing with rage. Twisting free from Trace's hand, I break through the fir branches and sprint back toward the palace. Images of what the Holy Guard could do to my whisperer sister overlap with promises of what I'll do to Trace for wasting precious seconds.

I pray to the stars that Leaf hid in the passage below our suite. *If* she had enough warning, *if* she moved quickly enough, *if* she was in the room at all, *if* the passage wasn't compromised. Too many ifs.

A body slams into me from behind, forcing me face first into the ground. Dirt and twigs grind into my skin, sliding into my mouth and nose as I gasp against the weight now on top of me. Trace's familiar musky scent identifies my attacker even before he speaks roughly into my ear. "You can't go back for her now. You won't make it ten steps before the Holy Guard cuts you down. And if you do, you won't make it out. The best thing Leaf can do now is hide or surrender, not race through battlegrounds with you."

I buck under his weight, glaring between the trees toward where I know the palace stands. "Not your call."

"It is when you can't think for yourself," Trace growls. His silver hair brushes against my cheek, a cruel mockery of the last time our faces were this close together.

"Go to hell."

Something sharp pricks my ribs. A knife. "You may come with us voluntarily or in binds," Trace says. "That is the only choice you have." I coil in on myself and slam Trace with the back of my head, the scrape of skin against his blade negligible beside the fury pounding in my chest. Trace grunts but holds. "As you wish," he says, seizing my wrists and twisting them behind me. The pressure on my shoulders forces me up to my knees. I hear a rip of fabric and Trace secures my wrists together, keeping my joints strained until the knot is secure.

"Let me go," I say, trying not to shout. My heart thumps against my ribs, my skin flushing with a toxic mix of rage and betrayal. "Let me go, or I'll tell everyone who you are. We'll see which of us ends up in binds once I do."

Trace leans down to whisper in my ear again. "Go ahead. How long do you imagine the princeling will live if his guards kill each other off?" Ignoring my curses, Trace marches me back into the tree-covered cove, the others staring wide eyed at my binds.

"Someone important to Kal is still at the palace," Trace offers by way of explanation. "He is having some trouble differentiating between 'planned rescue' and 'pigheaded killing-spree suicide.'"

Luca winces at my binds but nods understandingly at Trace's words. The angles of his normally smiling face look sharper in fatigue and fear; even his unruly reddish-brown hair looks tired.

I cut Trace to bloody pieces with my glare.

He cocks a brow. *Told you so.*

"I guess when you have experience leaving others to die, it's easier to swallow," I hiss at him, knowing I've hit my mark as his face settles into cold stone.

"This way," Trace says, motioning the group out the back end of our refuge. "The more distance we can put between us and the palace right now, the better."

We hike through the green silence for six hours, our quick pace hindered only slightly by Calvin, Alexa, and Jasmine. The sweet scents of sap and earth, once so comforting to my scout-trained nerves, now grate on my lungs. Every time I blink, I can see my sister, each image more noxious than the last. Leaf screaming while a guard drags her down the corridor, her crippled foot banging on furniture. Leaf dead, the blood from her slashed body soaking the palace's marble floor. Leaf chained and herded to Bahir. I vomit twice and make three attempts to flee, until Trace grabs ahold of my bound hands and force-marches me ahead of him. The rage blazing through my blood threatens to torch the world.

But the world could not care less.

Finally, Luca points out that with the setting sun and Calvin and the girls' growing fatigue, half our party won't be able to keep upright much longer. "I'm not sure we can call the escape successful if we kill them in the process," he tells Trace, who growls in reluctant agreement.

"We'll stop for the night. No fires." Trace tugs on my wrists. "Give me your word that you'll stay put, and I'll cut the binds."

"Cut the binds, and I promise to leave without slitting your throat."

"As you wish," Trace says, tying me to a tree. He pulls the binds tighter than strictly necessary over my chafed wrists. Luca surveys us with a weary glance and disappears into the woods to sweep the perimeter.

Sitting on the cold ground, I survey our motley crew. The campsite Luca chose is as good as can be found here, with a small stream for drinking water twenty paces off, a bit of rock-free ground to sleep on, and plenty of wide-branched trees to provide some shelter and concealment. Not enough to keep us dry should rain come, but better than nothing. Except for Trace, who is checking our scarce supplies, the others sit together in an exhausted huddle. The girls clutch their small bundles to their chests. Calvin spreads his coat over their shoulders, then leans down to massage his feet.

Wil stares into nothingness. I call his name softly, shifting into a more comfortable position. He turns to me, his wide eyes and pale face making him more ghost than boy. His blond curls are matted to his head with sweat.

"Are you all right?" I ask Wil.

"No," says Wil. "I imagine none of us are." He picks up a stick and begins to whittle the bark with the small knife he keeps in his boot. "Who did you leave behind?"

I lean my head back against the trunk. *Leave behind* sounds too final, too complete an action. With six hours between us and the assault, the truth of it hits deep. "My sister."

"I didn't know you had one." Wil's eyes stay on the curled pieces of bark beneath his knife, the blade continuing to move with a steady *swish, swish, swish.* "I left mine too. Though I don't think she would have come, even if she could have. In fact . . . I'm certain of it." His throat bobs, but he masters himself without shedding tears.

"I'm sorry," I say, which is stupid and inadequate, but all I have. "I'm sorry about your father too."

Swish. Swish. Swish. Wil's knife continues its whittling. "Do you want me to untie you?"

My jaw tightens. "I want the bastard who bound me to untie me."

Two paces away, Trace turns his head toward us. "Keep your voices down. We've enough trouble as it is."

The next hour passes in silence, broken only when Luca reappears with a report of a clear perimeter and a pair of cooked rabbits. The smell of crisped meat makes my mouth water—until the illogic of the meat's existence registers.

"Was there a merchant peddling rabbits in the woods?" Trace demands.

"There was." Luca grins, setting the rabbits on a stone. Taking out a knife, he hacks the meat into juicy pieces and holds the first morsel out to the girls. "She was pretty too."

Trace pierces Luca with a glare. "You caught and roasted a pair of rabbits without worrying that a fire would signal our whereabouts to anyone with eyes?"

"The rabbits were cooked when I caught them," Luca calls over his shoulder as he cuts the next small piece and holds it out to Wil. "Plus, did *you* see a fire?" The prince—I can't think of him as the king, not yet—looks at the meat blankly and shakes his head. "You should eat," says Luca. "No point in all this effort to keep you alive otherwise."

"No point in wasting dinner on someone who is likely to lose it," Wil's flaccid voice replies. Filtering out both the conversation and the overbearing aroma of rabbit meat, I tune my ears to the sounds of the forest. A cold shiver runs through me. Warranted caution or reflexive paranoia, I don't know. But Trace is already doing the same thing, his eyes surveying the dark trees.

A movement in the periphery steals my breath.

Before I can utter a word, Trace snaps to one knee beside

me and slices his knife through my binds. He holds a hand out to help me up, his other extending a sword's hilt to me, the polished steel reflecting speckles of moonlight. I take the weapon but ignore the hand.

"It's a buck," says Luca warily, following the direction of our gaze. "I saw him wandering around. Look." Picking up a rock, Luca hurls it into the foliage. Something rustles and runs.

I nod, though my heart fails to slow. Luca hands me my ration of rabbit, which I swallow without tasting. The buck's rustling sounds over and over in my head, my pulse jumping each time. I've missed Viva Sylthia's approach once. I can't risk it again. A hand reaches for my shoulder and I spin, my sword in my palm, before I see that it's just Calvin.

"Don't touch Kal," Trace tells him.

"Apparently not," the older man murmurs.

The heat coming off my face could warm the entire campsite. "Of all people, Trace, you are the least qualified to offer humanitarian advice." I take a breath. "My apologies, Master Calvin. It's been a—" I cut off midsentence and spin back to the woods. Something is still there. Watching me. Getting ready to pounce, now that it's dark.

"Kal?" I'm uncertain who speaks, but it quickly stops mattering as a patrol of six men rush us with weapons raised.

2

KALI

*T*he girls scream but I feel calmer than I have in hours. With the adversary finally before me and a sword in my hand, I can forge my own outcome instead of waiting for it to spring upon me from the shadows. I feel rather than see Trace at my back, his muscles flowing with the lethal grace he takes for granted.

The six-man rose patrol splits into pairs, four men going after me, Trace, and Luca, while the remaining pair heads straight for Wil.

The shift of Trace's weight is all the signal I need; he wants me to move closer to the prince. Before I can oblige, the first attacker is upon me, his face concealed in his hood's shadow. I parry the sword aimed at my gut, the force of the blow rattling my still-healing bones. The man winds his sword over his shoulder, readying his next strike. He has the advantage of strength and reach, and his eyes say he knows it.

His sword falls in a sweeping arc. I throw myself to the ground, staying beneath the deadly blade. The moment it passes over my head, I spring to my feet, only to block the next blow. And the next. My balance wavers. The man grins, his white teeth flashing in the moonlight. With his next attack, the sword slips in my sweaty grip and I fall to my knees to keep hold of the blade.

A thread of true fear twists in my gut. I'm a decent swordswoman, but nothing approaching Trace or Luca. Half-healed, exhausted, and lacking my throwing knives, I'm little more than a nuisance in the attackers' path.

Had I gone after Leaf like I wanted to, I'd be long dead by now.

Trace's sword stops a blow that would have split open my skull. The lack of reprimand stings like salt on raw flesh. Trace is proving himself more right with each of my failings.

Flushing, I jerk my mind back into the fight. Trace's parry has forced my foe's sword wide, creating an opening. I see the space, claim it, and slide inside. With my next breath, I'm close enough to inhale the attacker's scent, its familiarity stirring my gut. I block off my thoughts. With our bodies so near, the man's sword is useless. I must keep it that way. Must keep him from regaining space to swing his weapon. *Close. Stay close. Fight close.* Snaking my hands behind the man's neck, I snap his head down onto my rising knee.

A bone cracks. The man grunts. Warm blood running from his nose seeps through the cloth of my breeches. Before he can recover, I lift my knee for another blow.

He crosses his forearms to block the attack.

My knee strikes something hard and uneven beneath his sleeve. A vambrace with weapons. Knives. My fingers rip cloth, moving by feel to a weapon's hilt.

The man yanks his arm away, a single throwing knife staying behind in my palm. He wipes his ripped sleeve over his face, our eyes meeting for the first time.

"You?" His nasal voice is a punch to my gut. His eyes widen, the whites gleaming in the darkness of night. "Goddess. You. How—"

He never finishes. The throwing knife in my hand is *my* knife, and it flies true into the base of Nasal's neck. Bile rises and burns my throat, the obsidian wall of memory trembling in recognition of my captor. Nasal's body falls to the dirt, the shocked look frozen in death. I've the wherewithal to spin around and take the measure of the fight before lowering my guard.

The small alcove is littered with bodies, but the melee itself is finished. Wil stands with a bloodied sword in his hand, a man's corpse at his feet. Luca is bending over one of the girls, Jasmine. Trace holds the last living attacker against the base of a tree, a sword pointed to his throat.

I take the rest of my throwing knives and vambrace from Nasal's corpse and numbly strap it to my arm. *Don't think*, my mind orders. *Don't remember. Focus on now.*

"Samuels." Trace's clipped tone turns my attention to the prisoner.

"Aye." The man rubs his mustache, the mole at the corner of his mouth bobbing with the movement. "I wish I might say 'well met,' guardsman, but . . ." He clears his throat. "I imagine you are not inclined to release me, so I'd be obliged if you hurried up with my execution."

"Wait," I call, quickly stepping to Trace's side in case he decides to fulfill the request too quickly. My breath is ragged, but the words come clear enough. "How long have Viva Sylthia rebels been serving in the Holy Guard?"

Samuels chuckles. Trace presses the tip of his sword harder against Samuels's skin. "The boy asked you a question."

"I heard." Samuels spits blood onto the ground. "Kill me

or let me go, Trace. We both know those are the only choices you have within you."

Trace's nostrils flare. "What were your orders?"

Samuels raises his chin, exposing his jugular to Trace's blade. My jaw tightens, acid burning my throat. Soft footsteps tap the ground behind me as Calvin joins us.

"Sergeant Samuels, is it?" The older man leans on a walking stick, but his quiet voice carries an ice-cold edge that has Samuels's breath quickening. Smiling without humor, Calvin squats down to eye level with the prisoner. "I think you are quite right about the guardsman here—Trace can do little beyond end your life. Shortsighted of him, perhaps, but it's true. Just goes to show that professionals should stick to their own trades." He pauses, his voice dropping lower. "Speaking of professions, do you happen to know mine?"

WE LEAVE SAMUELS—WHO proved quite talkative when left alone with Calvin—tied to a tree. Grabbing supplies off the dead roses, we gather ourselves together and put as much distance between us and the battleground as we can before our strength gives out completely. According to the sergeant, his was the only patrol sent this way, though others will likely follow when the men fail to return. A small window of relative safety. Small and brittle.

We stay put for the darkest part of night and move out onto a mountain path with the first dawn rays. No one speaks. Trace's promise of a higher-ground advantage and a cave large enough to offer shelter is all that keeps us moving, however slowly.

Jasmine, her broken arm bound to her chest, stumbles so much that Luca passes his arm around her and half supports, half carries the girl along. Wil carries a sword. I carry my knives and the slimy sheen of my own uselessness.

The images of Leaf flash in my mind's eye again. An endless, exhausting loop of horrors, any of which might be real. Might be happening this very moment. Leaf. My fragile, brilliant, loving, thoughtful, defenseless Leaf. Alone and suffering, waiting for me to come for her, not knowing that I'm getting farther away with each step.

I couldn't go back for Leaf now even if I wanted to, and therein lies the greatest horror of all: In the pit of my gut, I *don't* want to. Because I'd die if I tried. I could barely save myself when Viva attacked, much less protect Wil and the girls. Stars, the prince took down as many attackers as I did. And I needed Trace's help. This isn't a scuffle in a remote town, where I decide if and when to engage. This is war.

"Here," Trace says, halting before an unimpressive mountain face amidst a thinning tree line. Before anyone can summon strength for a question, he moves several stones aside, revealing a crack large enough for a man to fit through. "It's one of the waystations on the path to Everett. Many whisperers have stayed the night here. We'll be safe enough."

Luca squeezes himself through the opening first and has a lantern glowing by the time I maneuver in after him. The cavern is large enough to house our group comfortably, its ceiling allowing me to straighten in the center, though Trace and Luca must stay hunched. A fire ring in the corner holds a few pieces of charcoal and a beat-up cooking pot.

"Stars," says Wil, twisting his slender frame in a full circle. His once-splendid clothing, accented with bits of velvet and subtle embroidery, is covered with caked dirt and dried blood. The prince's gaze is still glassy beneath his long lashes, but at least he is moving. Talking. "I never imagined a cave feeling more luxurious than the Delta Royal Palace."

Alexa and Luca help Jasmine inside and settle her onto a blanket. The girl's moans send my eyes toward Trace's neckline, where the depleted healing crystal hangs beneath his shirt, useless. If Trace hadn't had to use all its magic on me, Jasmine would be better now. Not that anyone but Trace and me knows he is a healer. Or that I—the guardsman trainee they know as Kal—am a girl named Kalianna.

"Master Luca?" Alexa's voice is thin as a thread. "Jasmine has a fever. I can't get her to drink any water."

Wil crouches beside Jasmine, brushing the girl's hair from her face, then looks up to survey Trace, Luca, and me. "I'm sorry," he says, his throat bobbing. "Not just for tonight, but for every day that I made the likelihood of you getting hurt to protect me more likely."

"Let's live through the day, then we'll talk," Luca says, trying for a hint of a smile and failing.

Wil nods.

Kneeling before the cooking pot, Calvin empties his pockets of the plants and herbs he collected during our trek. He selects several for the pot and pours our remaining water over the plants. I fetch the flint and start a fire for him.

"What now, Your Highness?" asks Calvin. In my fatigue, the duality of the address nearly makes me giggle. *Which prince did you want, Calvin—Dansil's or Everett's?*

Wil rubs the back of his head. "You heard Samuels. Bahir has declared Dansil a sanctuary of the Goddess and me a disciple of the Dark God. It appears he's been preparing this coup for a while now—the Order certainly took the capital with little effort. I imagine it will be some time before I can return to Delta."

"And do you plan to return, Your Highness?" Calvin sets the pot atop the flames, seeming for all the world to be fully engrossed in making tea rather than guiding a kingdom's ruler

14

through planning his destiny. I glance around the cavern, curious as to how many others picked up on the questioner's ways, and find Trace watching the prince intently, his muscles tense.

"Yes," says Wil, his voice ringing between the stones. The prince is just as sixteen as he was yesterday, but it's an older sixteen now. A harsher one. "Yes," Wil repeats, "but it will be a different Dansil and a different court." He pauses, drawing a breath, and surveys our little band, holding each of our gazes in turn. "And it will not start with friends held against their will. Trace, do not try to stop Kal from leaving again if he wishes. Or anyone else. You've all done more for me than I deserve, and you should make your own choice of path now. I've no expectations that you'll continue on with me."

Free to make my own choices. Never has freedom had so many shackles.

"Continue on with you to where?" Alexa asks from the corner.

Wil rolls his sword hilt in his hands and nods to himself. "Everett. They are no friends of Bahir's. Perhaps they will stand with me."

Trace snorts, straightening to as full a height as the cavern allows. "You are ready to hike to Everett alone?" he demands, whatever leash he had on his temper during the trek snapping like a dry branch. "Had you ever spent a night outdoors before yesterday, Your Highness?" He waves a hand in the air. "You think *one day* of reality has granted you some untold wisdom and skill?"

Wil puts down the sword and stands. Hands in his pockets, he rolls back on his heels and regards Trace coolly. No two men have ever looked more different. Smaller, younger, with a bit of feminine beauty beneath the grime and blood, Wil is a sapling bending in defiant survival amidst a storm. Trace is granite, solid and unwavering.

One a prince discovering himself a warrior; the other a warrior hiding his birth as a prince.

Wil breaks the stare-down first—not through surrender, but rather a shrug that dismisses the whole process. "I'll manage. Everyone else can do as they wish."

With nothing more to be said, Trace retreats into a brooding silence and the group beds down for the night.

3

VIOLET

Something was happening. Violet knew it from the sudden influx of acolytes into the abbey dormitories and underground intake rooms, and the hurrying Children, and the never-ending stream of work that left her no time to sleep or eat or rest. Each time she tried to inquire, her sisters' answers ranged from vague to condemning.

The Goddess triumphs.

Do your duty and leave others to theirs.

Ask Brother Joshua.

Each time Violet finished a task, a new one was thrust upon her. She supervised acolytes tuning small light crystals for sale; she packaged wilting carnations into bunches; she tallied the coin the fundraising teams had gathered. All important work, but none carried the urgency it was assigned. Or warranted sisters delivering food to Violet so as "not to disrupt your task with needless treks to the canteen."

Finishing filling the last of the empty baskets with an assortment of goods for the fundraisers to take into the field for sale the following day, Violet slid down the wall of the well-lit cellar until she was squatting on the ground. Her hands ached. Her eyelids drooped. And her stomach churned with a hated, too-familiar feeling of being disregarded as a bit of ornamentation.

Which was ridiculous. Each sister and brother who came with new assignments or sustenance spoke of Violet's work as vital to the Messenger and the Goddess. In the palace of her birth father, Violet had been needed for nothing. In the Order, she was crucial to every menial task. Especially today. Whatever today was.

They insisted there was nothing happening. Or at least nothing that Violet needed to know just then. The unease tying her insides into knots was fatigue, and the Dark God was using her weakness as a vessel for poison and doubt. Violet needed to return to the dormitory for a few hours of sleep, but despite the seemingly endless series of tasks, the call to evening assembly and prayer was yet to sound. She would not disgrace herself by sleeping while others worked, but perhaps a short rest away from watchful eyes would be forgiven. Getting out of the cellar before anyone arrived with a new task was simple expedience, not insolence.

At least, that's what Wil would say.

A pang of longing for her birth brother tightened Violet's chest. *The Dark God works through the ones we love,* she reminded herself firmly. That the thought had wormed its way so deeply into her mind was certainly the Dark God's work. Violet needed rest.

Holding her breath—which was ridiculous because she was doing nothing wrong—Violet rose and pushed open the door.

It failed to budge.

She frowned and pushed the door again, rattling it against

18

the engaged lock. Brilliant. Zalia, who was the last to see Violet, must have locked it on reflex. With valuables inside, the cellar had to be kept under lock and key lest the Dark God tempted a weakened soul to take the Goddess's things. Luckily, growing up with Wil had its unusual advantages, one of them being a solid education in beating locks.

A quarter hour of work later, Violet stepped out of the cellar and walked down the corridor of nearby intake rooms. Glancing through the slits, she found a room with an unoccupied patient chair and slipped inside the dank space. The darkness and discomfort were a fitting tithe for shirking work, and Violet immediately felt better about her deviance. She sat on the cold floor, resting her forehead on her knees while her eyes filled to the brim with warm tears that streamed silently down her face.

Something was happening. Violet *knew* it, just as she *knew* she was being kept ignorant by design. After fourteen years of not mattering in her birth home, she knew the signs. Zalia hadn't accidentally locked her inside the storeroom. She'd done it because the True Family didn't trust Violet the way they trusted others. Her royal birth made her different. It had always made her different.

"What's your name?" The thin voice sounding from a dark corner of the intake room startled a scream from Violet. "It's all right," the voice said quickly. "I won't hurt you."

Stars. The room hadn't been empty after all. Whoever left a patient here unattended and unrestrained was in for a world of trouble. Violet's heart sped, shaking off her fatigue. This was the Goddess's doing, leading Violet to this room just now. She took a calming breath. The smart thing to do would be to sound an alarm, get a full intake team here to deal with the girl in the darkness. But the Goddess had guided Violet here alone. It was a codex. A test. A way for Violet to prove both her trustworthiness and her skill by turning a patient into an acolyte by herself. With no tools but her voice and faith.

"I'm Violet," she said slowly. "I won't hurt you either. I want to help. What's your name?"

"Princess Violet?" The girl's voice sounded almost relieved. "I'm Leaf." She hesitated, then stepped out of the shadows in the corner. Despite being older than Violet, closer to nineteen or twenty, Leaf was small and fragile in stature. She wore a servant's dress, ripped and stained now—recent rips and stains, given the healthy state of the intact fabric. Leaf smiled kindly at Violet, putting forth a brave front in spite of the fear rolling off her in waves. "Do you know where we are?"

"In the Goddess's temple." Violet scrambled to recall how Zalia and Dasha had welcomed her into the True Family when she'd known nothing of the world. No brilliant words came to mind, so Violet went directly to the simple truth. "Two decades ago, the Goddess told the Messenger her plan to save us from the Dark God when the final battle comes. He's been working for our salvation ever since. Those of us here, the Children of the Goddess, are his soldiers, and these are our barracks."

The girl's face drained of blood. "You are one of them," she whispered, moving along the cell wall.

Violet's breath hitched in her chest but eased quickly as she realized that Leaf was moving away from her, not toward her. Moving oddly, too. Violet dropped her gaze to the floor just as Leaf gasped, stumbling against the wall on what looked like a twisted foot. No, Leaf posed no physical threat to Violet. The bum leg likewise explained why the girl hadn't tried to leave the cell despite the lack of restraints.

Violet held out her hand, palm up. "There is no need to be frightened," she said softly, as if talking to a wounded animal.

"We want to make the world a place where love rules, not violence."

"I was seized in the palace by the Holy Guard," said Leaf. "They asked each servant whether he or she wished to join the Order. Those who said no were beaten. Since they found me with a healing stone, they forced me here with the other whisperers. No one bothered asking whether I wished to join or not."

Violet's mouth dried. "The whisperers will be made acolytes," she said on reflex, her mind still processing the girl's claim of a palace assault. "They will have the chance to pay a tithe for their sins so that the Goddess can welcome them."

"Bahir's guards beat innocent people." Leaf's thin voice had fight. "When I was led here, we passed through the battle in the main courtyard. My escort was so frustrated to be missing the action that he separated from the convoy long enough to throw a knife into the Everett princess's face while she was trying to flee. There was a great deal of blood for a group that wants love to rule, not violence."

Violet's skin flushed. She lacked the facts for this conversation and felt it failing further with each word. Leaf was wrong. Whatever was happening aboveground, she'd misinterpreted the events. The Messenger had everything under control. His work was an instrument for everyone's good. "There is a good reason for what you think you saw, Leaf. I don't know what the reason is just now, but I know it's there. I'll find out for you, all right?" This was not how intake was supposed to go, but Violet's head was spinning more with each breath. "The Dark God is very devious, and it's up to us to evict him from our hearts."

"Yes, of course," Leaf said, her voice dulling. "You are right. It's all for the best."

Before Violet could help herself, the question she'd fought

so hard to ignore bubbled from her mouth. "Did you see King Firehorn or Prince William?"

"I've not seen your brother," Leaf said, settling herself into a corner as far from Violet as she could manage. "But the king's head sits on a flagpole in the palace courtyard."

4

KALI

I only hear the haggard breathing because I'm up to relieve myself and have headed as far away from Luca, who stands watch outside the cavern, as practical. Peeking silently around a tree trunk, I find Trace on his knees. He scrubs his hands over his eyes and sits back on his heels, gulping deep, desperate breaths. I take a step back as quietly as I can. Trace tilts his face to the sky, his hands shaking as he runs them over the spots on his legs where my bones were once shattered. I wonder whether the phantom pain that still haunts me claims him as well. Stars, what a nauseating web of violence and grief.

Silently, I return to the cave. I'm about to slink back into my shadowed corner when I see that Calvin is awake as well, sitting beside my blanket. He opens and closes his hand with pained slowness, while the others' soft snores promise that at least some of us are getting sleep.

"I fear the weather will turn soon," he says, turning his

hand over. "My joints are a more reliable indicator than I would wish."

"Is there anything I might do to help?" I ask, kneeling beside him. "My sister gave me a heat crystal, which can ward off aches. We could have Alexa tune it for us."

"I'll manage." Calvin pats my hand. "But thank you, girl. It was a kind thought."

The blood freezes in my veins. "What did you say?" I whisper.

"I said thank you. For offering a heat crystal."

My mood for games is nonexistent. "The other part," I hiss through gritted teeth.

A soft chuckle. "Does it matter right now, in the quiet of night?"

I lick my dry mouth, my heart still racing like a drum. "How did you know?"

Calvin shrugs. "It's my trade to learn people's secrets, to listen to their bodies and actions as much as their words." He touches my hand again. "Worry not. I keep what I learn to myself. Though I hope you'll soon find less need for the secrecy among friends."

I rub my wrists. They tingle with the memory of Trace's binds.

"You asked me an interesting question a few days ago, before you disappeared," says Calvin. "Do you recall it?"

I'd wanted to know whether people, the ones who survive, can recover from a questioner's methods. Calvin claimed it possible—with help. My thoughts stutter. "No," I answer too quickly, rising to my feet. "I'm afraid I do not. Goodnight, sir."

"Kal." The rebuke in Calvin's voice halts me in my tracks. "Your displeasure with Trace's choice to detain you by force is understandable. But his motives were well placed, if unkind. And this night, I do think he might value a friend."

Of course Calvin knows about Trace's current excursion. And that I found him. And that I left. I don't know why I'm even surprised anymore. I roll my shoulders before answering. "Trace is fine. He's just . . ." I shake my head. "He will little welcome company just now. Especially mine."

Calvin massages his wrists. "Want and need are not always the same."

I sigh. There is too much of my sister in the old man. It's easier to indulge the suggestion than to bear the guilt of refusal. "I'll go talk to him," I say. "But if our talking wakes up the dead, it's on you."

I retrace my steps to the discrete copse where I last saw Trace and find him gone. The waning moon casts scant light through the clouds, and even with my eyes adjusted to the darkness, it is impossible to make out a trail in the woods. Closing my eyes, I listen to the forest, half hoping I hear nothing to give me direction. Then I can return to Calvin and say honestly that I tried.

The rustling of leaves in the wind fills my ears, an owl's wise hooting mixing with the thin crackle of twigs as small animals scurry along. But there is another sound too. One that isn't native to these woods.

Whatever Calvin thinks about the goodness of Trace's motives, the fact is that Trace *forced* me away from Leaf. He took away my choice. Bound my wrists. The raw skin chafes against my shirt in reminder, sending a rush of anger through me, even as the faint sounds of a man moving through the darkness give away Trace's whereabouts. I follow the sounds, willing them to disappear before I catch up. If making Trace feel better is so high on Calvin's priority list, maybe he should have gone himself.

"Who's there?" Trace's voice demands, cutting off my hopes. Moonlight glitters off the steel pointing toward me.

I sigh and step closer, holding out empty hands. "Someone dumb enough to come after you."

The steel whispers as it descends into its sheath. "Go back, Kalianna."

"Walk me back."

A humorless chuckle. "I think you'll make it just fine. All of you will."

There is an odd finality to Trace's words, and I frown at his silhouette. Wide shoulders, straight back, hair shifting in the light wind. I cross my arms. "Are you going somewhere?"

"Yes."

"Where?"

"Away," Trace says calmly. Too calmly.

I walk forward until I'm close enough to feel the tension radiating off him, the moon casting dim light across his face and jaw.

"Of all things to come up with doing in the middle of the night after fighting a rose patrol and marching for hours, this rates somewhere between absurd and moronic," I mutter, taking hold of his elbow. The tightly corded muscles beneath the pads of my fingers send a familiar energy through me. "Let's go back to the waystation. We'll discuss whatever this is in the morning."

He stays rooted to the ground.

"You're serious?" It takes me voicing the words before I start to believe them. And once I do, my heart lurches into a gallop. Trace leaving is not a possibility I've ever considered, and I'm as unprepared for it as I am for the sudden vice of fear gripping my chest. "Stars, Trace, why? Where?" Realizing my voice is rising, I check myself quickly. "Is it Raza? Are you going back for her?"

Trace shakes his head. "If Raza failed to make it out with her guards, there is nothing to be done for it just now."

I frown. "Then where is it you so desperately need to be?"

"Nowhere," he says, as if that's an answer.

And it is, I realize. It's *the* answer. Trace isn't seeking a destination; he's just running. My fingers dig into his flesh.

"Coward," I hiss. He flinches but recovers, raising his chin, ready to accept whatever blow I plan to deliver next. I oblige. "We're setting course for Everett and it terrifies you. So you run. Like you did five years ago. Except this time, you can't tell yourself that you'll do more good implanted in the adversary's court, because that court just fell." I swallow. "So where to now? To find some new master to torment you? Some mystic tithe to wash away the sins of a seventeen-year-old boy?"

Trace's breathing quickens. "This from the girl who hides in the shadows when she should be eclipsing the sun?"

My face heats. "So a day ago I was doing too much in trying to rescue my sister, and now I'm not doing enough?"

"That isn't what I meant."

"Then what did you mean?" I ask in spite of myself.

Trace opens his mouth, closes it, and steps away, shaking his head. "Nothing. I don't mean anything. Go back to camp and then go to Everett."

Everett. Yes. The hurt bubbles to the surface of my memories, burning with hot, reason-defying fire. My hands tremble at my sides, but I'm beyond caring. Or watching my words. The narrow escape, the binds, the fight, the fatigue, they all join forces to feed the inferno in my chest. "That's what this is all about, isn't it? The only reason you've . . . paid attention, let me believe in some bond between us. You wanted me to go to Everett, and now that I'm on my way there, you have no more need to be around me." I tip my face up to the sky, cursing myself for the stupid little girl I turned out to be.

Trace steps up to me, his voice low. "You think I forced you from the palace because—"

"Because I'm a tool to you, one you maintain so you can point it in the right direction when you think it proper." My words come between heaving breaths. "I don't understand why you want me in Everett so badly, but that's been your goal ever since you discovered that I have some connection with magic, that I might pose a danger to Bahir."

I shake myself, thinking back to the night Trace found me in the wake of my capture by Viva Sylthia. I was broken. Dying. Trace found me, used his healing crystal to knit together torn muscle and shattered bone. But the healing hurt and I fought, somehow pushing the magic away from me and back into Trace. He told me about Bahir being a mage, someone who can manipulate magic directly—the only one on the continent. And then . . . then he insisted I go to Everett. His words return to me, vivid as ever. *If you won't go to Everett for your safety, then go to discover what your relationship to magic is. Find out whether you pose more danger to Bahir than comes from just knowing his secret.*

I meet Trace's eyes. "I was your mark, wasn't I?"

"You are insane," Trace says, towering over me, his broad shoulders blocking out the starlight. "I came looking for the broken pieces of you that Viva Sylthia left behind *before* I knew anything about your magic and the danger you might or might not pose to the bishop."

The logic of his words does nothing for my temper. "I don't know why you came after me. Not yet. But I'll find out. The prince of Everett would not rescue a worthless guard trainee without a reason."

Trace stills. "Worthless guard trainee?" He mouths each word slowly as if digesting its meaning. His hand rises to grip my chin, and his fingers, calloused from wielding a sword, scratch against my skin. Trace's dark eyes bore into mine as he speaks. "You are brave and loyal and beautiful. I dragged you from the palace because I'd rather live with your hate than with your death. And I followed you into the forest because . . ." He falters, his eyes slipping, losing their confidence. "Because when it comes to you, I seem incapable of rational thought."

5

KALI

*M*y body stills. I stare at Trace, half expecting him to laugh and declare it all a jest. My heart pounds against my ribs, the sounds of the forest suddenly too loud. Intrusive.

The owl hoots again, as if to say that she heard my complaint and little appreciates it.

Trace swallows, the apple of his throat bobbing. "Do you know how stupid it was of me? To run off, making no arrangements, waiting for no one, likely heading into the same trouble that caught you?"

Trace brushes his large palm over his face, rasping softly against the stubble that's grown since morning. There is a small scratch above his left brow, the blood dry now but still visible in the dim light. The vulnerability in his gaze flickers like a light bug.

I blink at him like that silly hooting owl. His words still race along my nerves, making my breath come quick, leaving me with too little air. He steps closer and raises a hand to cup my face this time, running the pad of his thumb along my cheekbone. My skin tingles where it touches his. Instinct, born of years under Lord Gapral's rule, screams at me to pull away. *This will end in hurt, in blood, in death, in pain,* a voice in the back of my mind hollers. *You know better.* Despite the chill air, beads of sweat soak my temples, and my legs tense, ready to run.

But something stronger keeps me still, even while my heart races as if trying to match the rhythm of his. From the twitch of Trace's face, I know he feels the pounding in my chest as vividly as I feel his. His silver hair, unbound tonight, cascades over his face down to my shoulders, cocooning us together. In a trick of the moonlight, a speck of silver shimmers in his eyes as well. His body's lean muscles, whose movements my body has learned from training and shared battles, are still as night now. His free hand rises to cover my galloping heart.

"Don't leave us," I whisper, so quietly I can barely make out my own words. "Don't leave *me.*" A sharp intake of breath.

Closing my eyes, I lean into the warm hand he still holds to my face. It smells of steel and salt. I breathe deeply, savoring his scent, determined to burn it into my memory before it's gone. Trace's thumb caresses my cheek again. A touch so gentle, it should belong to a butterfly instead of a deadly warrior.

Heat rushes through me, starting on my cheeks and running down the back of my throat, my chest, the inside of my thighs. All the fibers in my body want *more.* Even as I'm terrified by *more.* Even as I don't know what under the stars *more* looks like.

Just that I want this heat to last forever.

Trace's thumb touches my lips, sending a new wave of energy cascading through me.

I open my eyes, meeting the dark intensity of his. "Rune," I whisper.

He flinches at the name, but instead of pulling away, he leans closer to me. "Yes," he breathes, his body taut with the same energy that has woken my senses. My mouth parts, moving of its own accord as my heart stutters.

Trace's nostrils flare delicately, as if he's taking in every sense of the moment. His hand slides from my chest to cup the back of my head. His face dips, his lips so close to mine that the phantom tickle of their touch brushes my skin.

My hands wrap around his waist, my nails digging into his back.

Trace growls faintly, the sound rumbling with a deep, feral possessiveness that awakens my body to every smell, every line, every touch that is him. His lips brush the corner of my mouth, his body trembling with restraint. My grip on his back tightens, my body demanding—begging for—his touch, even as remnants of fear pulsate through my veins. The brand on my shoulder throbs in memory of Lord Gapral's lessons. Of consequences.

Trace's tongue caresses my lower lip. Teasing and questioning. A tongue that knows exactly what it's doing, if the tingle rushing through my body is any indication. A small moan escapes me, and his mouth finds mine, sealing the sound between us.

The press of his lips is soft only for the heartbeat it takes me to press into his touch. Then his mouth pushes hungrily against mine.

The energy waking my body moments ago is nothing compared to the explosion that sears through me now. An impossible mix of terror and pleasure. I taste the steel and wind that is Trace, each press of his tongue igniting a new flame inside me. My essence trembles, volatile as black powder.

My nails press into his skin. Trace's other hand moves from

my face to brace the small of my back, his hard body both unyielding and protective as he holds me against him.

We pull apart violently, our burning lungs demanding the breath they've been denied too long. Panting, I stare at Trace, who is frozen too, except for his heaving chest. Cool air rushes between us, sending a tremor through me. Fear and desire whisper to me in unison. *What have you done, Kali? What will you do now?* My face heats as my body proposes an answer. The stiffness of Trace's shoulders betrays his own struggle to reclaim mastery of his blood.

"What do we tell the others?" I ask finally between ragged breaths.

"You can start with the truth," Luca's harsh voice says from a few paces away. "And go from there."

6

KALI

*H*eart pounding in my throat, I spin toward Luca, whose glare threatens to burn down the forest. I scramble to calculate how much he might have heard, but the reality is that I've been blind to the world since first finding Trace.

Beside me, Trace clasps his hands in the small of his back and straightens before Luca. The silence rips me to shreds. My mouth is dry, my body too cold with Trace's sudden absence. Luca's condemning stare strips me naked, and I wrap my arms around my shoulders.

Luca jerks his head toward the cave. "In fact, why don't you tell us all."

Trace shifts his weight.

Luca's hand slides to his sword hilt. "That wasn't a request, *Highness.*"

"Luca," Trace says quietly.

"No." The storm in Luca's eyes shows just how little

provocation it would take for him to draw steel. And blood. "Shut your mouth and walk."

Moving slowly, Trace shows his friend his empty palms before carefully drawing his blade from its scabbard and holding the weapon's hilt toward Luca.

Luca snatches the sword, its edge leaving a deep cut in Trace's palm.

Trace wipes the blood against his shirt and presses the wounded palm against his forearm. "I pose no threat to you, Luca," he says quietly. "Let me leave."

My breath catches, an abyss of ice opening inside my chest. *Let me leave*, a voice chuckles hideously inside me, parroting Trace. *Me*, not *us*. The full extent of my miscalculation lashes across my face like a whip. *I warned you*, the voice says. *You've no one to blame but yourself. What is it you imagined was happening, little fool? Love?* Bile rises into my throat.

Luca's lip curls. "Get back to the cave, Rune. We may wish to sell you to Everett for their assistance."

"Luca," Trace starts again.

"No, traitor." Luca points Trace's own sword at his heart. "Walk."

I sit with my head bowed as Luca recounts every intimate detail that Trace and I shared in the dark's deceptive privacy. In the light of the fire, sleepy faces stare from their blankets. Alexa and Jasmine, plainly confused as to the implication of Luca's words, hug each other in fear. Wil and Calvin sit forward, weighing every revelation.

Leaning against the cave wall, Trace listens with a face of cool indifference, while each word Luca utters is a blade slicing into my soul. The only doubt his recounting leaves is whether I am an Everett accomplice or Trace's plaything.

"Would you like me to weigh in on this," I ask Luca once he wraps up the recitation, "or are you satisfied with your own personal account?"

Luca turns to me, his mouth twisting. "By all means, enlighten us, Kal. Or whatever your name is."

I raise my chin. "My name is Kalianna and I am a trained scout that King Firehorn brought in to help understand the threats he might be facing. By living as both Kal, a male guardsman trainee, and the royal Lady Lianna, I was able to get access to a greater number of places then either persona alone would have allowed."

Luca raises a brow. "The king brought you in to protect him, and upon discovering that his personal guard was an enemy spy, you proceeded to crawl into said spy's breeches instead of reporting treason?" He snorts, shaking his head. "You'll forgive me when I say that you may have been better off keeping your mouth shut just now."

Put that way, I can't exactly disagree.

I draw up my knees. This isn't how my second-ever kiss was supposed to end. Not with humiliation and tears and utter aloneness. Lord Gapral never expected celibacy from his scouts, but he insisted that all pleasures of the flesh be acquired and paid for through his vetted network of courtesans. No entanglements. No mixed loyalties. I should have taken Gapral up on the offer to make the arrangements. Maybe then, these misplaced moments with Trace wouldn't be tearing my insides to shreds. Maybe I'd have known better than to kiss Trace in the first place.

"At least we won't be coming to Everett as emptyhanded beggars," Luca finishes, glaring at Trace. "The only question is whether we'd do better presenting him as a goodwill offering or granting his life in exchange for assistance."

Wil and Calvin trade uneasy glances, but I can't tell

whether their dismay is rooted in the notion of selling Trace as a commodity, the practical difficulties of holding him hostage, or the general unpleasantness of spending time with an Everett spy.

Trace clears his throat. Even hunched over in deference to the low ceiling, he appears oblivious to either the hurtful words or the horrid plans. "One problem, Luca," he says now. "Prince Rune has been dead for five years. How exactly do you imagine an Everett commander will respond to your claim that I am said corpse?"

Calvin raises a finger. "Who is aware of your . . . lack of death, Your Highness?"

Trace exhales. "My parents. My sister. Present company."

I press further into the wall, the words reaching me through a fog.

"The envoy knew nothing?" asks Wil, speaking for the first time since Luca's announcement.

"Envoy Jajack came into service after Rune's death," says Trace.

"Convenient," Luca says, his nostrils flaring.

"No. Designed." Trace turns to him. "I was seventeen and thought I knew better than the generals. I took a lot of men on a fool's mission that ended very badly—enough to jeopardize the people's faith in the throne. Rune's death controlled the damage."

"A prince whose stupidity kills his men is a disgrace. A prince dying at the enemy's hands is a call to unity. Was that the theory?" asks Calvin.

"Yes. My father went to great lengths to ensure that Rune's martyrdom stuck. Those who knew me well soon found themselves in other posts," Trace continues. "My sister's appearance in Dansil's court was, well, *unexpected* is an understatement." As he answers Calvin's question, Trace's eyes remain on Luca. "Ask what you want to know."

Luca's back stiffens and it's a few heartbeats before he manages the words. "All those plans and patrols you put in place in the name of safeguarding Firehorn, all those times I came with you because I trusted you—what were you really doing? What were *we* doing?"

"We were safeguarding Firehorn," Trace answers immediately. "Each and every time."

"Because you're a loyal Dansil subject?" demands Luca.

"Because I am loyal Everett subject," Trace shoots back, pinning Luca with his glare. "Because Firehorn was the bridge to peace with Everett. The only bridge." Silence settles over the cave as Trace's words hang thick in the air.

Jasmine moans. Glancing at the young girl, I realize she must have given in to the fever sometime during the conversation.

Alexa scoots to her friend and touches her sweaty forehead. "She's burning," Alexa says quietly. "Badly."

Luca pushes off the wall and kneels before the prone girl, cursing softly under his breath.

Alexa sobs.

"Rune," Luca says after a moment, his voice strained like a bow as he breaks the silence. "You healed Kalianna. I heard you say it. What do you want in return for healing this child as well?"

My heart tightens.

"I can't heal her," Trace replies.

Luca is on his feet in an instant. "Because she does nothing for your cock?" He spins to me. "What did you do for him to *earn* a healing?"

One moment I'm sitting against cold stone and the next I'm on my feet, my fist swinging hard into Luca's jaw.

7

KALI

*L*uca's head jerks back, a bit of blood trickling from his lip. His eyes flash, his right hand cocking over his shoulder, the knuckles aimed at my lip.

I throw up my arms and—

A pair of hands grips me from behind, wiry arms hauling me away as Trace tackles Luca to the ground. I struggle to join them.

"Stop, Kal," Wil's voice commands in my ear.

I let my hands drop slowly, my body shaking. My breaths come in short, heaving bursts.

In front of us, Trace now straddles Luca, pinning down the man's wrists. "You don't raise a hand to her," Trace shouts into Luca's face. "Or I will rip your eyes out myself and feed them to the hogs. Understand?"

"She did strike him first," Calvin points out, staying well away from the fray.

Trace twists toward the older man. "And you think that makes it all right?"

"I think none of this is all right, Prince Rune," Calvin answers calmly. "Starting with the fact that, of the seven escaped survivors of the coup, one is blazing with fever and three are brawling like cats in heat. If you might kindly release Master Luca and explain why you will not heal the child, I believe we would all value the insight. I presume that healing does not, in fact, have anything to do with the patient's desire to procreate."

Trace snarls once more at Luca, then jerks himself away and walks up to me. "Are you all right?" he asks, his fingers touching my elbow.

Wil wisely steps away.

"Of course not." I wrap my arms around myself and glare at Luca, who is watching me warily, tugging his disheveled clothes back into place. "Trace can't heal Jasmine because he used all the power of his only healing crystal to save my life after Viva Sylthia captured me. I understand that your preference would be different, but we can't exactly change the past."

"Captured by Viva?" Luca repeats.

"That's what I just said. Is there a bloody echo?"

Trace touches my face, his eyes finding mine. "You don't owe him a story," he says softly.

"Like hells she doesn't," Luca says.

Calvin clears his throat. "Master Luca, what is it that has you so homicidal just now? The fact that an Everett prince concealing himself in King Firehorn's personal guard decided against revealing his origins to you? Or that a scout followed that same king's orders instead of telling you who she was?"

Luca's jaw tightens. "They didn't seem to have a problem sharing as much with each other." He sighs and slides down the wall until he's sitting on the ground, his head in his hands. "Bishop Bahir is a violent traitor who murdered my king. The dead Prince Rune of Everett has been protecting Prince Wil, the son of Everett's chief enemy. And the boy I've been training to fight is a girl who doesn't need any guard training because she is a scout. I don't bloody know up from down anymore."

"You think that's bad?" Wil says, settling beside Luca. "Try getting a throne and losing it in the same two minutes."

Luca shuts his eyes, pinching the bridge of his nose. "Stars. Wil—"

"Don't say it." Wil's words are clipped, his forearms resting on his bent knees. His gaze finds the ground, drilling into the hard-packed earth. The cave falls quiet for several heartbeats until a low sound from Wil's throat rumbles through the air. A sound suspiciously close to laughter.

"Wil?" I say, feeling Trace's heavy hand on my back.

The prince's shoulders shake, his quiet laughter bouncing through the cave. "Oh, stars."

"Your Highness?" Trace says quietly. "What—"

"Sonia." Wil snorts, the laughter bubbling from him in earnest. "At the Wandering Dog. I was thinking of the Wandering Dog, when Luca hired a girl for Kal."

A corner of Luca's mouth twitches. "Kal looked like a startled rabbit. I thought I was doing a good thing, you know." He glances at me, just a touch of the eyes, but a touch nonetheless. "What did you do with her outside?"

"A gentleman doesn't discuss such things," I tell Luca.

His smile widens. "Is this why Trace stopped training with Kal all of a sudden?"

Trace crosses his arms. "I don't hit women."

"Actually," Wil raises a hand, "I believe you hit them just fine. Unless it was another Kal you whipped in the North Wood."

Trace pulls his arms around himself. "I didn't know."

"I believe that particular oversight has been remedied now, no?" says Luca, sending Wil into another absurd burst of maniacal and slightly infectious laughter.

At least laughter is better than murder.

WE SPEND what's left of the night in uncomfortable sleep, Calvin suggesting that we might wake feeling better. Stronger. I can't help wondering whether I'll wake up to find Trace gone.

Trace does not, in fact, disappear under the cloak of darkness. Neither does fatigue nor humiliation.

My limbs are heavy as I go through the motions of checking weapons and bootlaces and supplies, my eyes occasionally straying to Trace and never finding him looking back. When we finally move out with the morning sun, I carve out a quiet place for myself at the head of the group, where I can look forward and see nothing but trees.

"So, what do I call you?" Luca asks, matching stride with me after two hours of silence. It's slowly getting chillier the farther we get from Dansil, and I wager that evergreens will outnumber the other trees in a few days' time.

I squint to block out the sun's rays as I judge our path, calculating whether Calvin and the girls would do better with a longer, flatter trek or a shorter uphill hike. It's easier to think about the forest than about what's happened.

Luca clears his throat and I realize he's still waiting for an answer.

"Kalianna," I say, steering us toward the flatter path.

"No," Luca drawls. "That won't do. Too many syllables."

"What?" I turn to face him finally. "It's my name."

"Don't you have a better one?" Luca sticks his hands into his pockets. "What do your friends call you?"

My jaw tenses. "Scouts don't have friends, Luca. We have marks."

Luca makes an uninterpretable sound in the back of his throat and walks beside me in silence for another dozen steps before speaking again. "What I said last night was unforgivable. But I apologize nonetheless."

I turn my face away, my skin heating anew. Beside me, Luca kicks a flock of pebbles down the path, the small stones skipping and singing when they hit bigger ones. Scout, Luca is not.

"Stars, Kal. I'm an idiot," he says softly. "Ten kinds of idiot. You were right to slug me. And if I were in Trace's shoes, I'd have taken my head off for me and shoved it deep into my ass. Then again, it might be there now."

Trace. What does it mean that Luca, not Trace, is here talking to me? Does Trace regret kissing me? Think me an added complication in an already too-complicated existence?

"How is everyone holding up?" I ask. *Is Trace as aloof as I am this morning?*

"As well as can be expected," says Luca. "Jasmine is weak but Trace says this course will take us right to an Everett fighting camp. He hopes some of the men might be superstitious enough to wear healing stones. And if not, then a magic-free healer will do."

So Trace is active and strategizing. Relief and anger hit my gut together. For a heartbeat, I can think of nothing but how warm he tasted, how he smelled of the forest and sweat and steel. And how small and inconsequential a kiss must be in the life of a prince, even one fallen from his kingdom's grace. I brace myself to ask my next question. Luca is hardly the ideal person to ask, but I've no one else. Never have. "Luca?"

"Mmm?"

"How many women have you kissed?"

He looks sideways at me. "I don't keep notches, Kal."

My face heats but I press the point. I need to know what's normal, what importance people who are not me place on that touch of lips. "A handful? Ten? More?"

"Stars, Kal, couldn't you have asked me that before I knew you were a girl?" He blows a strand of hair from his face. "Dozens. Maybe more. I'm considered quite talented by most ladies." He shifts uncomfortably. "You weren't looking for . . . er . . . advice, were you?"

"No!" The heat beneath my cheeks turns to flame. "I mean, I'm sure you'd have good advice but I think I'll little need it." I close my eyes. "That sounded wrong. I just mean, thank you—you've told me what I needed to know." Dozens. No doubt, Trace has explored as many lips, women he's tasted and forgotten.

A kiss is nothing to those who aren't me.

8

KALI

"*L*ianna." Wil lengthens his step to walk beside me. We are on day three of the hike, and if everyone else gets quieter by the step, the prince won't stop talking. Usually Luca, Calvin, and Alexa bear the brunt of the chatter, but apparently today is my turn.

"The others are calling me Kal," I say, glancing down at myself to ensure that my breeches and tunic haven't suddenly morphed into an evening gown. They haven't.

"Not all others." Wil sticks his hands into his pockets. "Trace is calling you nothing at all, it seems."

I grind my teeth. "Is there—"

"Are you my sister?" Wil asks, the question spilling from his lips as if held under pressure. "I thought Lady Lianna was my cousin. If you are her . . . Was it true, about the relation? Or just something my father made up for the courtiers?"

I rub the back of my head. I hadn't considered the now-obvious question before, which means I must stumble through an answer on the spot. *When all else fails, try the truth.* "I am the bastard daughter of the late Lord Firehorn, your father's younger brother. But any possible claim I might have to the throne has been legally dissolved, if that's a concern."

Wil laughs without humor. "It isn't. In fact," he waves his hand in the air, "consider it undissolved."

"I don't think you can just undissolve it, Wil."

"I'm the uncrowned king of Dansil," he says darkly. "I can do whatever I want."

I snort.

A corner of Wil's mouth twitches. "So you *are* my cousin."

"Bastard cousin, if you'd like to be technical."

"I wouldn't like to be technical," Wil says. "I'd like to be family." He gives me a shy sideways look. "If you'll have a dethroned ruffian for a relation."

A tickle of unexpected warmth spreads through me and I squeeze Wil's shoulder, stopping suddenly with my fingers still digging into his flesh. "Wait. If I recall, when you thought Lady Lianna was your cousin, you spent a good deal of time positioning buckets atop her slightly ajar door."

Wil kicks a stone down the path. "No wonder you never fell for it. Kal was bloody standing right next to me."

I chuckle, letting go.

"You said you had a sister," Wil says, his voice quiet now, and I realize that, unlike me, the little bugger gave this conversation a bit of thought beforehand. "The one you wanted to go back for when the coup happened. Can you tell me about her?"

I bite my lip, my chest tightening to suffocation. "Her name is Leaf." The words hurt as they come out. "And she might be dead now."

"She might be alive too. Tell me about her?" he says again. "I'd like to imagine I have a big family, even if just for a little while."

The evening comes quicker than I expected, my voice slightly hoarse from speaking as we settle around a fire, Trace sitting as far away from me as the space allows. Despite the past days, the forsaken kiss still encircles my heart like a thorny collar, threatening to bleed me dry if I make a wrong move. I wonder whether he blames me for his forced return to Everett, since he was about to run when I waylaid him in the woods and unknowingly led Luca right to him. Every time I gather myself to ask, however, I find the moment not quite fitting.

Drawing a breath, I get up to feed the fire and find a place right beside Trace after placing the log in the crackling flames.

Trace rises. "I'm going to gather some poles to make a litter for Jasmine," he says, looking away from me. "I don't think she will be able to walk much longer."

My chest clenching, I mirror Luca's nod as if I'm somehow a part of this decision and smile weakly at the rest of the party, who remain sitting.

"So, what are you two fighting about?" Wil asks once Trace walks out of hearing range. He pokes the fire with a stick, waiting patiently for my answer.

My face flames and I quickly raise a canteen to my lips.

Alexa elbows the prince in the ribs. "Don't ask that," she says with all the deep knowledge of a twelve-year-old. Calvin coughs quietly and excuses himself to check on Jasmine.

"Why not?" Wil twists to the girl. "It's not like they are being subtle about it. Why should I feign being an idiot when they really *are* idiots?" Wil frowns, scratching the back of his head, his voice suddenly serious. "Am I supposed to beat Trace up?"

The water in my mouth expels in a sudden fountain, and Luca pounds my back as I reclaim my airway. "What the bloody hells are you talking about?" I ask Wil, once I can breathe again.

Wil frowns. "Isn't that what brothers do? I wasn't a very good brother to Violet, and I want to get it right this time." He pokes the fire again. "It's just that I'm rather certain Trace would kill me if I punched him."

"You aren't her brother," says Luca.

"Given the lack of familial availability, I think cousin is close enough," Wil replies.

Luca extends his long legs toward the flames, crossing one ankle over the other. "If Kal were my cousin," he drawls, "I'd tell her that a man who follows her into Viva Sylthia's clutches and kisses her like Trace did cares about her very deeply."

I squirm in my seat, weighing the option of burning the lot alive against the effort it would take, and finally deciding to surrender instead. "And what would you tell this cousin about why this man might insist on ignoring her after said kiss?"

Luca grins. "I'd say said man is likely trying very, very hard to keep his cock in his breeches." His grin widens to match my blush. "Maybe too hard."

"Or maybe," Trace's low voice behind us makes Luca and me both jump, "said man is aware that we will cross the Everett border imminently, at which point he will become an entirely different person from the one you all think you know." Dropping the poles he found onto the ground, Trace stalks to an empty place by the fire and sits down. "Now, if you all are so intent on philosophizing this evening, we should cover a few points more relevant than my cock."

Luca is the first to speak, blinking innocently at the thunder incarnate now sitting beside us. "What in the world could be more relevant—or interesting—than your cock?"

Trace growls. "We can start with Bishop Bahir being a mage, Kal being a magical anomaly, and Alexa being able to tell us what the Order of the Goddess does with the whisperers it captures. Let us exhaust those topics initially and then go from there."

We are still on that discussion three days later when we cross the stream that demarks the Dansil–Everett border here and find ourselves held at sword point by a well-armed patrol.

9

KALI

"Name yourselves," demands a tall uniformed man around Trace's age. His sword is free of its sheath and glistens menacingly in the sun. His four companions, all with equally sharp swords held in trained hands, surround our group with deadly calm. I tense as Trace and Luca slowly lower Jasmine's litter and raise their empty hands. Despite purposely heading toward the Everett camp, having the patrol ambush us is bloody unsettling.

Wil steps forward, his back straight and face dirty. "Prince William of Dansil at your service, sir," he says, executing a perfect court bow. "And what's left of my court. Might I have the honor of meeting your commanding officer?"

The men exchange amused looks, but their commander gives Wil an appraising glance. "I am Lieutenant Copa," he says, returning the bow. His sword point diplomatically lowers a few inches but still remains poised. "Might I inquire as to the reason for your presence here . . . Your Highness?"

Wil runs a hand through his hair, looking more like the boy

I remember. "I realize you've no reason to believe me, but can we agree that our band poses a threat to nothing but a clean shirt?"

Copa raises a brow but nods, a small chuckle escaping his professional expression. With a signal of his fingers, the men sheathe their blades.

"Thank you," says Wil, closing his eyes with a sigh. "Now, I imagine that no matter what I say and claim, you've some protocol for what to do with us?" He scratches the back of his head, his voice sheepish. "We were rather hoping to find you, instead of the other way around. It would have made for a better entrance."

"Quite so," Copa concedes. "But as you said, we have protocols that make the particulars of how this encounter came about matter little. If you would follow us to Camp Vanguard, I'd be much obliged."

"Of course," Wil murmurs as if there is a choice in the matter. Copa gestures with one arm and two of his men step forward to take up the poles of Jasmine's litter. Copa is anything but a fool.

My heart speeds as we hike the rest of the way, but I manage to stretch tall as we enter the war camp itself, keeping my chin up, my gaze straight ahead. Anything I can do to create the appearance of confidence that I feel none of. Our plan, if this desperation deserves such a word, is to convince King Owain to support Wil's claim to the throne and back that support with armed forces. For starters, this means looking more like worthy partners than scared children.

Unable to help myself, I steal a glance at Trace. However uncomfortable the entrance is for me, I know it's a hundred times worse for him. But his steady gait and calm face give away nothing. Which is infuriating.

From the stares of Camp Vanguard's soldiers at our

procession of ragtag invaders, I'm certain we've failed to create the first impression we wished for. The Everett soldiers, on the other hand, look every bit the part of a well-trained army. Clean and orderly and similar, the men share Trace's dark eyes and light hair. Shades of blond and silver locks, cut short and neat, are abundant. As are people. Young, vibrant, strong. *Stars.* I've not the slightest idea how Dansil ever thought we could match Everett in combat. Or in anything else. The Everett army has not stepped foot onto Dansil soil, yet I already feel conquered. Or conquered *again*, since Bahir has laid his claim to Firehorn's throne.

Trace's gaze slides to me for the first time in days, and it's all I can do to keep from grabbing his hand like some helpless little girl. But stars, I want to. I want to feel his warmth and his strength and know that I am not alone, in a way that only touch can say. I want it so badly that my heart races and my fingers twitch at my side. I hate myself for the want. The need. Especially since Trace's interest in me, if it ever existed, seems to have changed course the moment our lips touched. Much like our first kiss, which disappeared the moment it was over, like Trace took a great broom and swept it from his memory.

"Are you all right?" he whispers.

"Fine."

He turns toward Wil. "This is a large camp. Looks like one of the forward divisions. The commander will be a lesser general."

"Is this a good thing?" Wil whispers back.

"Yes. It will be simpler to have decisions made with a ranking officer in charge. It also means military rules will be observed to the letter." Trace's gaze returns to me and stays, waiting for something.

"And one of those rules frowns upon women taking up arms, doesn't it?" I guess, quickly adding a bit more boyish swagger to my stride. The last thing I need is to be separated out. Trace nods, his eyes leaving me immediately. As if it would kill him to speak to me more than necessity demanded.

Lieutenant Copa stops before a large tent. The guards posted outside snap to attention, touching their weapons and hearts. Copa excuses himself from us and ducks inside. Left without their commander, the other soldiers circle us in one silent, coordinated movement.

"General Hewe will see you now," Copa says, emerging from the tent. "I apologize for the inconvenience, but I must ask you to leave your weapons outside."

Despite his perfectly polite tone, I know there is nothing apologetic in the request. Just as I know that, though we've been permitted to keep our swords until now, one of Copa's elite warriors would have had a blade at the throat of anyone reaching for steel. I surrender my sword; Trace, Luca, and Wil do the same.

Trace leans down toward me, his heat mixing with mine. "Your throwing knives too." I give my head a minuscule shake. *No. Not my blades.* Trace growls softly. "They know you have them." Indeed, raising my eyes, I see several of the soldiers waiting on something. Copa smiles politely. Gritting my teeth, I unstrap the vambrace. Taking it off leaves me feeling naked.

"Thank you," says Copa crisply. "This way, please. Your injured companion may remain on the litter. I've sent for a medic and I give you my word that no ill will befall the girl while you are inside."

Luca hesitates but there is little choice. With Wil leading the way, we enter the general's tent. Large and well lit, the space is set up for holding counsel. Maps cover the canvas walls, a table holds wine and is surrounded by matching chairs, and a clerk sits ready with pen and ink in the corner.

General Hewe rises from behind his desk. For an instant,

I'm thrown back to Firehorn's study on my first day in the palace. Thick with muscle, General Hewe has a mustache, intelligent eyes, and the weight of many lives plain on his shoulders. His light hair is swept back from his face like Trace's and his uniform is cut finely, though lacking any embellishment. "Your Highness Prince William Firehorn." The general bows with no hint of mockery or surprise. Either he figures us for crazed imbeciles not worth contradicting, or detailed reports of the events in Delta have reached his desk a while ago. "Welcome to Camp Vanguard. Please allow me to extend my deepest condolences for your father's death and my outrage at the takeover of your rightful throne by an imposter."

Well, that conveniently takes care of the entire opening speech we prepared for Wil, who swallows and seems to shrink into himself without moving a muscle. "Thank you, sir," he manages after a moment.

Hewe sits, motioning for us to do the same. "You appear startled, Your Highness," he says with a tilt of his head. "What welcome did you expect when you set course toward my forces?"

"I expected you to require some proof beyond my word that I am who I claim," Wil blurts. Blushing, he shifts his weight in his chair. "Not that I don't appreciate it, sir."

General Hewe lets out a deep, booming laugh. "I like your bluntness, Your Highness. It is refreshing when dealing with the ruling class, if I might be so bold as to say so. Before you believe me too daft, allow me to return your bluntness with my own. First, however," the general snaps his fingers, summoning a footman to pour us wine, "allow us to indulge in a bottle that I've been waiting for an excuse to open. The grapes come from a small vineyard east of here and are picked just as the frost settles. I hope it suites your palette."

I watch the amber liquid burble delicately into my glass and take a slow sip, catching the clean, sweet taste that marks potent alcohol beneath. The wine is no accident. Especially on our empty stomachs.

Luca drains his cup dry in one gulp. Wil wraps his hands around the goblet but keeps it on the table, though I'd wager his hesitation has more to do with fear of shaking hands than with consideration of the alcohol's effects.

General Hewe takes an indulgent sip and looks around the table. "I promised to explain," he says, picking up his former train of thought. "As you are doubtless aware, an Everett delegation was in Delta proper when the coup started. I am pleased to report that they arrived safely at Camp Vanguard two days ago. Their description of the members of the Dansil royal family were collected as a matter of principle."

Raza. I dare not look at Trace, but sitting beside him, I feel the loosening of his shoulders and the slow, relieved exhale of held breath.

"Envoy Jajack should be joining us any moment." General Hewe watches Wil's face as he speaks. "In fact, I believe I hear him now."

As if on cue—perhaps deliberately so—the tent flap flies back to admit the envoy's familiar face. Everyone smiles politely, commencing a triangulated evaluation of Jajack watching us, Hewe watching Jajack, and us watching everyone together.

"Your Highness," Jajack says after a moment with a bow to Wil, "I am pleased to see you well. How might we be of service?"

Wil pushes the wine aside, his jaw tightening. For a heartbeat, he stares into Jajack's eyes so intently that I'm certain his mind is elsewhere. But then Wil swallows and draws himself to full height. "The day before Bahir's attack, you

58

came to an agreement with my father. I believe leaked news of this agreement precipitated the coup. I now ask for Everett's help in reclaiming my throne in order to honor the agreement made before my father's death."

I stiffen, looking between my companions, who seem as ill-informed as I am of the situation. Even Trace stares at Wil with widened eyes.

Jajack smiles thinly. "The situation has changed so greatly, Your Highness, that His Majesty King Owain must evaluate the request himself. I will have a dispatch sent at once."

"Why are we entertaining this lot?" demands a familiar voice a moment before its owner storms into the general's tent with a host of bewildered soldiers at her heels. "Should they not be in a cage somewhere?" Raza finishes, coming to a full stop beside the general.

At least, I believe the girl standing before me is Raza. With one eye and half her face hidden behind a bandage, it's hard to recognize the once-gorgeous princess in this wounded, furious creature. The perfect posture and flowing gait are also gone, replaced with hunched shoulders and painfully forced bravado. Her hands, nails broken and bitten to the quick, fold into fists at her hips.

Trace's sharp intake of breath is covered only by the scrape of chairs as the room rises to its feet. Tension crackles like lightning.

General Hewe's face takes on the color of Raza's scarlet brooch, sending the soldiers on her tail into a panicked retreat. "Your Highness." His glare finds the princess's uncovered eye. "To what do we owe this pleasure?"

Raza's hand sweeps over us, skipping over Trace with no more consideration than she granted the dirt floor. "I asked, sir, why these *enemies of the Everett throne* are without shackles."

"The Dansil delegation poses no immediate threat, Your Highness," Hewe answers curtly.

"This *Dansil delegation* left Everett people to be slaughtered like cattle in the middle of the Delta Royal Palace." Raza bares her teeth. "The next best thing to ordering our deaths themselves. You give them honor they've not earned, General."

"I give them military courtesy." Hewe's cold voice would send any sane person into hiding, but Raza seems beyond caring.

"I was under the impression that military courtesy applies only to members of the military. Have these refugees turned into an army while I wasn't looking?"

"Your Highness—" Jajack begins, but Raza cuts him off with a raised hand.

"Envoy Jajack, your authority ended when the mission to Dansil did. I remind you that you are now but an advisor to the throne, of which I am the sole representative in Camp Vanguard. General Hewe," she spins, facing the military man head on, "this is a political matter, not a military operation. I demand you cage these animals at once, on charges of assault against my person just over a week hence." Raza surveys us, her lips pulled into a tight line as if she is searching for something. Someone. When her gaze finds me, she steps up close and studies my face very, very carefully. When she speaks again, Raza's voice is deathly soft. "And General, this is a woman masquerading as a man. One of Dansil's trained spies. Have her separated out, chained, and questioned."

VIOLET

*V*iolet raced through the corridors of the Order's underground. Her breath came in ragged, uneven waves, her vision blurring at the edges. Her limbs caught on the occasional brother or sister who appeared in her path, like clothing tangling in thorns. She paid them no mind. Coming to the door of Brother Joshua's office, she leaned her shoulder against the thick wood and shoved.

The unlocked door swung open. The office stood empty. Violet spun on her heels and sprinted away, aiming toward the suites she'd visited only once.

More people appeared in her way now. Voices called her name. Hands reached. She dodged them all. Skidding to a halt before the Messenger's sacred rooms, she shoved her shoulder against the door the way she had at Brother Joshua's office.

It was locked. The living crystals studding the doorframe cast gorgeous arcs of color that seemed out of place beneath the ground. Violet had eyes only for the red. The color of blood and fury. She banged on the wood with her first. "Open the door!" she shouted, ignoring the pain in her hand. "Open—"

The door opened and Brother Joshua's disapproving face appeared before her. "What in the Goddess's name—" he started to say, letting out an *oomph* as Violet tried and failed to push past him.

"Calm down, one and all," the Messenger's deeper voice sounded from within the chamber. "Is that Violet, Joshua? Let my Child inside."

Joshua obediently rotated aside, giving Violet a direct line to Bishop Bahir.

She walked forward. Behind her, the door shut with a deafening click. The Messenger's suites looked even bigger than they had last time, the miniature Eye of the Goddess glowing like the sun. The fight that had carried Violet through the corridors like a crazed animal waned.

Bahir stood and extended both hands to her. "What's happened, Child?" he asked kindly. "Tell me."

Violet's mouth was dry, the words refusing to form. This was the Goddess's own Messenger standing before her. She loved him. And he loved her. This was folly. It had to be. The bishop dealt in love, not death. He knew nothing about her father's murder. The news would shock him, as it had her. If that whisperer girl's words were even true.

"My father—" she started, and the Messenger smiled.

"I'm here, Child."

"No," she shook her head, "my birth father. King Firehorn. Is he . . ." Words failed her. *The king's head sits on a flagpole,* Leaf had told her. But the girl was a whisperer, still tainted by the Dark God's touch. She was lying. She had to be lying. "Is my birth father well?" Violet asked finally.

"He is," Bahir said immediately, guiding Violet to a plush sofa.

Relief flooded Violet's body. She sagged against Bahir, the tears suddenly breaking free of their well and flowing freely down her face. The rich fabric of Bahir's long robes soothed her skin. He stroked her hair. Violet struggled for control of her voice. "Can I see him?" she managed finally.

"Easy, easy, Child. I've the greatest of news to share with you." The Messenger's hand came around her shoulders. "Brother Joshua and I were just discussing it when you joined us so fortuitously."

Violet closed her eyes, praying for the Goddess's forgiveness. She should have known Leaf's lie for what it was at once. But Violet hadn't; she'd doubted the Goddess's chosen. She deserved the horrid minutes of panic she'd felt. But the penance was over now.

Violet took a shaking breath. "You've news, Father?"

"You know that the Dark God once had a powerful hold on King Firehorn. You've known for some time now, sensed it in your blood. You even felt the tipping point of his soul and spoke to me of it. The Goddess guided your hand. Do you remember?"

She nodded warily. "The conversation with the Everett envoy, you mean?"

"That was the tipping point, yes. The greatest of dangers. From that moment on, I worked tirelessly to save Firehorn. The Goddess stays with all of her children, and while there is hope, I fight for each life. I prayed. We all did." He gestured with an open palm at the other man. "Brother Joshua held a vigil for King Firehorn's soul. Was that not good of him?"

Violet spared a quick glance at Joshua and mumbled, "Thank you." Her muscles tensed again.

Bahir smiled. "The battle for King Firehorn's soul was a hard one, Child. But I am pleased to tell you that we were victorious in the end. King Firehorn accepted the Goddess into his heart and she welcomed him to her. They are together now."

Violet blinked through her tears, not quite understanding. "My birth father is with the Goddess?" she repeated.

He smiled again. Nodded. Ice shredded Violet's heart. Her father was dead; that's what Bahir meant. And Violet was supposed to celebrate the salvation of his soul instead of mourning the loss of his body.

Dead. Dead. Dead. She'd trusted the Messenger and he'd allowed her father to die.

"How did he die, exactly?" Violet breathed.

"By the Goddess's hand," Bahir's tone chided. "What more do you need to know?" He sighed. "I feel your uncertainty, Child; I hear the questions the Dark God seeds in your thoughts. You must fight them, Violet. Do not let evil slip into your heart and darken your eyes now. Use your mind. The sacred knowledge I've granted you. Would you wish for your birth father to suffer in the underworld, or to live in the Goddess's embrace? Tell me."

Violet swallowed. "The embrace, of course."

"And if your birth father wanted to give his life to save his soul and his country, would you tell him to stop?" Bahir demanded. "Would you sabotage his chance at salvation and damn his kingdom to punishment and evil's triumph? Tell me."

The ice in Violet's heart dripped into her veins. "I'd want him happy," she told the Messenger. "Him and all of Dansil."

The Messenger smiled. "Of course you would. I know your heart is pure and that the call of the Goddess is strong in you. And so did your birth father. He died for a very important reason—to allow you to bring the Goddess's love to the people of Dansil. King Firehorn finally saw that which the Dark God had denied him seeing; he saw *you*, Violet. The bright, pure, vibrant girl destined to save all of Dansil."

Ice. Violet was ice and snow and cold. She had no feelings. What manner of Goddess put a head on a spike?

Bahir squeezed her shoulder. "You know that you are vital to the Goddess's work, do you not, my Child? You know how smart you are? How much your faith matters in the final battle between the Goddess and the Dark God?" Violet could only nod without thought. "Of course you do." The Messenger rose, straightening his robes. "I think you've spent too little time in the sun. Tomorrow you and I shall go back to the palace. Brother Joshua will arrange to have your things moved."

Violet stiffened. No words came. But no feelings either. That was good.

"You will not be alone," Bahir promised quickly. "You will never be alone again, my Child. I will stand by your side."

The words that should have summoned comfort brought only a void. "What about my brother?" her voice asked.

Joshua and Bahir exchanged glances. "I fear the news on that front is not as fortunate," said Bahir. "Prince William fell into the Dark God's lure. We have people searching for him as we speak."

"And then what?"

Bahir frowned. "We will show him the truth, of course. About the Goddess and the Dark God and the coming battle."

A shiver ran down Violet's spine, but she wiped the back of her hand across her face and stood. "If the king is with the Goddess and Wil is gone, who sits on Dansil's throne?" she asked, straightening her dress the way Bahir had straightened his own robes.

ALEX LIDELL

"The throne belongs to the Goddess now," said Bahir. "As her Messenger, I will translate her will for the Dansil people." A smile. "And you, Child, will take your place by my side, a princess leading the people of Dansil by example and devotion."

KALI

The soldiers who take hold of my arms are gentle—until I see the tent at the north side of camp, far enough away to muffle noise, and start to struggle against their grip. Stupid and pointless, but I can't help it. My mouth is dry, my palms damp. My legs feel as if they could run for leagues if just given a chance.

The soldiers haul me inside, ignoring my attempts to bury my boots in the ground. Metal manacles close around my wrists with a deafening *clank*. A chain is measured from each of them to a stake driven into the rock floor.

Trace let them take me, and they did. The obsidian wall in my mind trembles. The world around me darkens as if fog has rolled over the sun.

"Prisoner secure," a soldier reports to Lieutenant Copa.

"Very good." Copa turns to me, his eyes smoldering. "No one appreciates being deceived, Mistress Kalianna. Least of all the Everett army." I sink to the ground. A numbness spreads from my chest. I cling to the void for fear of losing what little control I have over myself. Copa sighs and checks my chains and manacles. Satisfied that all is in order, he leans out of the tent. "The prisoner is secure, Your Highness. You may enter."

Raza? I've only a moment to wonder what the broken girl wants with me before she enters in a flurry of skirts. The bandage covering her eye has shifted and the tail of a jagged red scar, running like a rat's tail down her cheek, is startling against her sallow skin.

"Leave us," Raza snaps at Copa. When he opens his mouth to protest, the princess rounds on him. "I thought you reported the prisoner secure, Lieutenant. Is she, or is she not?"

"She is."

"Then I wish a private word."

Copa brings his heels together in a salute. "My men and I will be just outside, then."

"Fifteen paces away," Raza counters. "When I say *private*, I do not mean I wish for the illusion thereof." Copa stiffens. I do too. "One more thing, Lieutenant." Raza extends her hand. "The wand, please. That wasn't a suggestion." Copa's face flushes, his eyes darting to me once before he unhooks a leather pouch from his belt and holds it out to the princess. The moment the leather leaves his hold, he motions for the soldiers to follow him out. They do, all avoiding my gaze.

Very deliberately avoiding my gaze.

Raza squats in front of me, just out of my reach. "I knew you'd be somewhere here, Lady Lianna. Once I saw him, I knew," she murmurs and unties the pouch, pulling out a wooden dowel with a crystal the size of a small walnut worked into a setting at one end. It looks like a flower, except that the crystal is black and opaque. "Do you know what this is?" she asks.

"I presume it's some breed of living crystal," I say with an evenness trained into me over a dozen years. "Though I've never seen a black one before."

She twists the flower between her fingers. "It used to be a healing crystal. They are powerful little things. So much potent magic compressed into such a small gem. But this crystal is dead now, its walls but a shell that will neither give birth to additional magic nor refine what's inside. Do you know what unrefined magic feels like? It is difficult to describe the effect. Here, let me show you." Swinging the wand forward suddenly, Raza jams the crystal against my skin.

I hit the wand away.

No. I *try* to hit it, but my muscles fail to obey.

My mind is just registering the shock of paralysis when the pain comes. A sudden infernal burn that coats my nerves in searing oil. I try to scream but the muscles to open my mouth and make the noise ignore me. My body convulses, flailing in violent silence on the ground. My lungs burn, desperate for air that won't come. My vision darkens. Raza pulls the wand away and steps back.

Breath. Sweet, wonderful, easy breath. I gulp air hungrily. My heart pounds, sweat forming at my temples and running down my cheeks. Raza squats to my level again, holding the wand out of reach. "It's called a stim crystal. The effect varies slightly based on the breed of living crystal it starts out as, but you comprehend the general idea. I imagine you've not seen one before. In a country that kills off its whisperers, you'd have no one advancing the field."

"What do you want?" I rasp.

Raza's face darkens. "I want to know what you did to my brother to make him choose your life over mine."

"What?" The fog of shock hangs thick around me, but I try to make sense of Raza's words.

"I was in the palace gardens when the Holy Guard

attacked Delta. Three of my guards died within minutes." She takes a breath. Delicate fingers reach up to touch the bandage on her head, her uncovered eye losing focus. "I waited for Rune. Searched for him. I was certain that only death would keep my brother from coming for me, from seeing me safe from rogue blades. But it wasn't death, was it? It was you. He chose to bring you to safety over me. When I saw him today, I knew to look for you nearby. How right I was."

I shake my head, humorless laughter bubbling inside my chest. If Raza bothered to watch her brother for more than two moments, she'd know that Trace is through with me.

The wand twitches in her fingers. A wave of fear rushes through me. "He didn't choose me over you," I say quickly. "There was no time to choose. It was happenstance. We happened to be in the same room when the coup started. That's all."

"It wasn't happenstance," Raza snaps back. "He left Delta to look for you, to bring you back. That is why you were in that same room of yours. And when the violence started, he saved you. Not me. I saw you all run, you know."

I'd explain it if I could. If I understood any of it myself. But I don't, so I gather the words I know to be true. "He loves you, Raza."

"Not enough." She stiffens. Her eye refocuses on me. With deliberate care, she reaches behind her head to untie her bandage.

My breath catches, bile rising high in my gullet. I swallow. Look away. Swallow again.

A deep, guttural growl escapes the girl. "It was a knife," she says. "A knife thrown into my eye. Then dragged out." Stars. I steady my breath as Raza covers her face again. *Stars.* "Say something, whore," she demands of me. "What lies did you feed him to allow this?"

"Your wounds are the fault of Bahir's terror mongers, not Trace," I rasp. "He couldn't have stopped that knife."

Her nostrils flare. "He could have healed my eye!"

"No." I shake my head. "A knife to the eye would have—"

"He could have healed me!" Raza shouts, spittle flying from her mouth.

I pull back, heart beating fast. My hands come up with a loud clank of chains, palms out. "All right," I breathe quickly. "You know better than I."

She takes a breath, which I take as a positive sign. "Your companion is badly wounded," Raza says, her tone sounding too normal for someone who's so clearly crazed.

I choose my words as carefully as berries amidst thorns. "Her name is Jasmine. She has a fever."

A hint of a smile. "She might die."

Stars. "She might."

Raza tilts her head. "So why has your loyal *Trace* not healed her?"

My heart beats hard, struggling to understand the direction of Raza's thoughts. "His healing crystal is depleted," I tell her.

She nods and I'm immediately glad I told the truth. She knew the answer before she asked. She leans in, bringing her face just outside the reach of my chains. "How did it get depleted? Not healing me, clearly. Who did Trace choose to save? You?" Her lip curls. "Did he heal *you*?"

I stay silent, which seems less provocative than confirming the sin aloud.

Raza rocks back on her heels and, before I can scream, presses the wand into my neck.

Knowing what to expect does nothing to lessen the shock of convulsing muscles. Through the haze of paralyzing pain, I see Raza adjust her hold on the stone, shoving the whole wand down the front of my shirt. With no more need to hold on to the crystal, she stands and retreats to the other side of the tent to adjust her clothes.

My seizing muscles scream their agony, but it's the burn in my lungs that sends waves of true panic through me. No air. I have no air. I am choking. I will die.

I strain to shift my body away. My muscles ignore me. Across the tent, Raza's back is to me. I'm going to die and she won't even notice. She will turn around, whenever that crazed brain of hers deems it right, and will stare at my dead body like a child frowning at a bug that splattered beneath her shoe.

My vision darkens, the world swaying around me. I long for the calm stillness of the shadows. Drowning must be like this. Unable to breathe, unable to scream, unable to fight. Some who drown breathe in water before they perish. I understand them now. A last chance to fill the lungs is so very tempting.

Tempting enough that I give in to it. Except it's not water that enters. Nor air. It's magic.

KALI

The oily magic flows into my lungs, my muscles, my skin. A coalescence of agony and bliss.

My body yields to it. Absorbs it into its pores. The fire blazing inside me turns to welcoming warmth, the magic a tangible thing. A familiar feeling surfaces, a memory. Magic has been inside me before, when Trace healed my injuries. That magic was different, still oily but refined and purposeful. The healing magic, tuned by Trace and filtered through the living crystal, had a mission. This magic is raw and untamed. It moves without purpose or direction. Stinging bees who don't know where to settle.

Like the wild magical tufts inside a novice whisperer's crystal. Except *I* am the crystal and the whisperer, both.

I grope for the words I've heard Leaf recite to novices, words she tried to recite to me in her trials. *Concentrate. Feel the magic's chaotic movements. Now envision how you want it to weave together. Coax the outermost strands toward the middle.* I guide the bees. Not with any muscles I've used before, but with another power inside me, one that is clumsy and uncertain from lack of use. I push, pull, coax. The roaming magic makes me scream in pain one instant and writhe from its tickling touch the next.

But I am screaming, I realize. I am writhing. I am breathing. I am moving. I am alive.

I take deep breaths. I stroke the bees lovingly. They are together now, but they want something to do. They want a purpose. They would like to make something whole, but doing *anything* would be better than doing nothing.

Calm. I need to stay calm. Closing my eyes, I imagine myself in the safety of the shadows. There are no shackles, no pain, no hateful eyes watching me writhe like a worm. I imagine myself absorbing the light around me so only darkness remains. I breathe in the darkness and breathe out the fear. In and out. Even the stinging bees seem soothed by the rhythm. In and—

The scream that shatters the tent should have belonged to me, but I'm fairly certain I was inhaling when it sounded. Opening my eyes, I find Raza pressing her back against the canvas wall. Her one eye is so wide with panic, I can see the white around her iris glistening from across the tent.

"What's going on in here?" General Hewe's deep voice booms from the tent's entrance. Copa, Wil, and Trace file in after him and stop dead. All of them. Staring at me with eyes as wide as the princess's.

Following their gaze, I look down at myself and choke on air.

Darkness as thick as night covers me like a blanket. Bringing my hand up to my face, I can't see even the outline of my fingers. Yet the people standing just a few paces away are crystal clear. As if I'm looking from inside the shadows into a lit room.

"Kal!" Trace screams, wheeling about to face Raza. He advances on her like a predator. "Where is Kal?"

"I'm here." My voice sounds too loud, my heart beating so quickly it hurts.

Trace spins back around, braces himself, and plunges into the darkness around me. His hands connect with my knee and shuffle quickly to my face. Warm, calloused palms touch my cheeks and smooth my hair. His forehead presses against mine. "Stars. Are you all right?" His voice is quiet, desperate. "Talk to me."

"What did you do?" Copa demands of the princess. "Where is the wand?"

"What did *I* do?" Raza screeches. "What did that whore do?"

Trace's hands roam down my arms, stopping at the manacles locked around my wrists. He growls. His hands move on, feeling the instrument beneath my shirt. He grips the wand and unceremoniously chucks it across the tent, then pulls me into his chest.

The crystal is a dull gray.

"Bloody stars, it's depleted completely." The horror in Copa's words ripples like lightning through me. "That's enough magic to kill ten men."

Trace's hold around me tightens. "You used a stim crystal on her?" The rage rumbles like thunder. "How dare you!"

"Enough!" General Hewe's voice booms over Trace's. "The stim crystal has its uses in questioning. It has no business in untrained hands. We shall address both of those issues once someone tells me what the bloody hells I am looking at right now."

"A mage acting on instinct," Trace growls toward the general.

"Then *un*-instinct it. Now."

ALEX LIDELL

I shudder at his tone, even as that word—mage—ricochets inside my head. My body curls in on itself. Mage? No. Bahir is a mage. I'm just an oddity. An anomaly of magic.

Trace's hold tightens. His forehead presses against mine again, his hands on either side of my head. "You are using magic to bend light into darkness, Kal. I need you to stop," Trace whispers to me, the thunder beneath his voice so violent, I can feel its vibration. "Control the magic, and yourself."

"How?" My voice trembles. My stinging bees, my magic, it wants to be *doing* something.

Trace draws a breath. He doesn't know. My blood races, washing my insides with panic. How could he know? He's a whisperer, not a . . . a mage. The mere fact that I absorbed and used an ex-*healing* crystal's magic to manipulate *light* contradicts the whisperers' principles. *Here is a corollary for you, Leaf. If you manage to extract magic from a crystal and feed it to a mage, a lot of things can happen.*

"All right," Trace's calm interrupts my panic. "Take a breath. Can you feel where that magic is now?"

I close my eyes, matching my breathing to Trace's. I feel the stinging bees inside me. "Yes."

He exhales. "Good. Can you release your hold on it? Stop directing it?" His words flounder for a second, synonyms being offered like keys in hopes that one will match the lock. "Wall it off?"

The last one feels right. The way I visualized myself absorbing the light, I imagine a hive forming around the bees. As the beehive's edges harden, my darkness—my glorious, safe, wonderful shadow—starts to ebb. I halt, my body trembling in Trace's arms.

"Keep going," Trace whispers softly. "You must show the general that you control the magic, not the other way around. If you can't—" The words catch in his throat, but I

76

understand. I just absorbed enough magic to kill a squad of soldiers. If the general deems me too volatile, he may order me put down like a rabid beast. I allow the beehive cocoon forming around my magic to mature and harden, cutting off the bees' interaction with the outside world.

Around the tent, gasps confirm my success before I dare open my eyes. When I do, Trace's dark ones are only inches away. Our breaths mingle.

"Princess Raza," Wil's words cut the air as he throws all the authority of a would-be king behind an adolescent, still-forming voice. "Attempting to murder a member of my court is an act of war. Unhand her at once."

Raza raises her chin. "Last I checked, Your Highness, our nations *were* at war. It is you who come here begging for peace and pity. As for the member of your court, as you put it, I find it insulting that you attempt to deceive my people by pretending she is anything but what she is."

Wil steps toward her, his chest forward. "Lady Kalianna is my cousin, a close member of the royal family. I demand you unhand her at once." I smile despite myself.

"Or what?" says Raza. Her head cocks to the side. "You demand I unhand her or you shall do what, exactly?"

Trace gives my shoulder a final squeeze and rises, coming to stand beside Wil. "Or," Trace's low voice rumbles through the tent, "your day will turn out worse than you can imagine, sister."

13

KALI

*T*he tent is mute. The general's and Copa's confused glances clash with Raza's sudden frozen silence.

Raza swallows. "Whatever do you mean by that, sir?" Her hesitant stuttering morphs into indignation too slowly. A moment faster and she would have had the power of incredulity on her side. "How dare you—"

"That is enough." Trace crosses his arms and towers over his sister. Calm. Strong. Too large for the constricting tent. "What's happened to you, Raza? What in the stars' name are you doing?"

She retreats a step, strikes the canvas wall, and recoils from it with a snarl. Her good eye glistens with silver tears. "So *now* you are back? After five years of hiding and war? Not for me, not for Everett, but for this . . . this harlot?" Raza waves her hand in my direction but keeps her attention locked on her brother. The hand hanging at her side trembles.

"First, her name is Kalianna," Trace says.

ALEX LIDELL

Raza crosses her arms. Her question hangs in the air like a lit fuse.

The memory of Trace's calloused hands cupping my face in the darkness echoes through my heart. Our foreheads touching, our energy merging into a whole greater than either of us alone. Then another memory. One outside a cave in the darkness of night, when I asked Trace to stay with me. And he did.

For the first time since hearing Raza's accusations, something inside my chest stirs, tentatively wondering if the princess might be right. That Trace did choose me.

Trace's gaze darts to the floor. Then to his sister. "Second," he says in a cold, powerful voice, "I am back because I cannot permit the woman you've become to sit on my people's throne."

Reality's chill percolates through me. Trace—Rune—is the crown prince of Everett. Of course his kingdom's welfare, not some girl, guides his hand. And certainly not a girl who masquerades as a boy and conjures darkness. He told us all as much around the campfire, said outright that the man who entered Everett would not be the Trace we thought we knew. I raise my chin, force a smile, nod along.

General Hewe pinches the bridge of his nose. "My tent, if you please, Your Highness. Both of you. All bloody *three* of you."

"My cousin—" Wil starts to say, but Hewe is already a step ahead, nodding to Copa to open my manacles. The relief I should feel when the metal falls away never comes. "It's all right now," Wil says softly, offering me his hand. "They can't hurt you anymore."

Apparently, I'm not the only one good at deceiving myself.

"Follow me, please," Copa instructs, leading me back

80

through the camp to a large tent where Calvin, Luca, and Alexa are waiting.

The old me, the Kali who left Lord Gapral's estate, would be counting soldiers and steps as we walked, but I can barely keep the ground from swaying beneath my feet. What does it mean that I'm a mage? Might it be a temporary condition? No, of course not. Even I know that much about magic.

Copa clears his throat and I realize I've not been listening. "I said that, for the safety of both you and the Everett soldiers, you may not wander the camp without a male escort. The same is true for the other females in your party."

"I don't believe Jasmine will be doing much wandering just now," I say dryly.

Copa nods politely and leaves.

Inside the tent I find a table with a pitcher of drinking water, a platter of dry bread and cheese, five chairs, and a set of pallets with woolen blankets. Taking one of the chairs, I recount what happened to the others, but I can only barely pay attention to their discussion. Luca is speculating whether Trace always planned to reveal himself or made a decision at the spur of the moment, while Calvin wonders whether Bahir might have suspected the full extent of my powers. And I count the seconds until I can be out of this place and as far away from Raza as my feet will take me. When Wil and Trace finally return to the tent, my palms are sweaty with anticipation.

"Well?" I ask, rising to my feet. "Do you know where King Owain is? When are we leaving?"

"We aren't," Trace says flatly. "A message has been sent to the king, and we are waiting for a reply before we may leave the camp. A soldier will be posted outside the tent to ensure that no one harasses you while you are here. Raza included. The men may walk around camp so long as you do not handle weapons or approach any locations where weapons might be stored."

My eyes shift to a sword strapped to Trace's waist. Apparently, the disarming didn't apply to him. In fact, with his widespread shoulders and clean shirt, he seems to have already changed from the man I saw not two hours ago. More regal, with wisps of power flowing off him, making him equally more aloof and attractive. Tantalizing. My heart stutters.

"Are we prisoners?" I ask, my chest tightening when Trace's full attention finally turns to me. "Because staying in a place with guards and no weapons feels a great deal like prison."

Wil takes a chair beside me, his face low. "We are guests," he says bitterly, making the word sound like an insult.

"You are not just guests," Trace says. "There is also the matter of who—or what—Kalianna has turned out to be. We'd thought Bahir was the only mage on the continent, but seeing what Kalianna did with that stim crystal, we were clearly mistaken."

"Can we talk?" I say, crossing my arms. "Alone."

For a heartbeat, I'm certain that Trace will say no, but he nods his head to the exit and walks me several paces from the tent, acknowledging the saluting Everett guard with a dismissive nod. His sharp, intelligent eyes survey the camp even as I open my mouth to speak. As if he is doing many things at once and this conversation with me is just a small branch of his responsibilities. A delicate, sinister pain creeps through me at the realization that *that*—my demotion from relevance—is very likely exactly what's happening.

I swallow. "Trace."

"Rune," he says softly, his face a mask of resolve mixed with a hint of apology. "Or Your Highness."

I take a step back.

Trace—Rune—no, *His Highness*—follows. "All choices have costs, Kalianna. I did not ask to come to Everett, but I am here now. And it is how it has to be."

My hands are cold as I bow my head and shoulders crisply. I will *not* let him see the slap his words delivered. "You've called me a mage several times now, Your Highness. I'd like to know what the bloody hells that is, exactly. What it means. How I control it. If it's Your Highness's damn pleasure that I don't cause some catastrophe by accident, Your Highness might be required to condescend to speak with me."

A sigh. As if he isn't the one driving this dance. "Given that you've been a mage all your life and have never caused a catastrophe before, I believe the camp is safe enough," Trace —Rune—says dryly. "Having studied Bahir, I can tell you that mages don't generate magic themselves, but rather draw it from a source. I did not realize your nature when I healed you because the reaction was small and reflexive. In the incident earlier today, however, you clearly manipulated the magic your body ingested. You made the magic your own. Used it. Speaking of which, I meant to inquire as to whether any of the magic you absorbed in the prisoner's tent is still contained inside you."

Incident. Is that what we are calling Raza's torture now? I school my face. "It is." A cocooned beehive buzzing in a space it found for itself. Somehow living both in and outside of my body at the same time. I've tried to avoid thinking about it. Childish, perhaps, but too much is happening already without reliving nightmares. "I feel like a human living crystal now." I'm uncertain why I bother adding the latter.

Rune nods, unsurprised. "I imagined the same analogy. Though a crystal's nature stays constant, whereas you were able to use the unrefined magic of a healing crystal to manipulate light." Clearly, Rune has given this more thought than I have. "Perhaps your eventual spectrum will come from the combination of the type of magic you absorb and the manner in which you are able to channel those magical reserves."

"Have you any notion of how I might go about *absorbing* magic, short of stim crystals?"

"No. But no need to get ahead of ourselves." Rune straightens his tunic. "I would like you to start training the way a novice whisperer would. Do the basic exercises, attempt to tune the magic that is within you. Perhaps the translation of skills will only be partial, but anything that might prevent an uncontrolled instinctual outburst is beneficial."

A bloody royal decree. I want to shove Rune on his princely arse. I wonder whether training with Prince Rune will be as delightful as working with the captain of the Dansil Royal Guard, Trace. Regardless, it appears our relationship has come full circle and we are back at meeting for the first time. "All right," I say finally. "Your schedule is the busier one. When would you like to start?"

"Work with Alexa," Rune says, turning to leave. "It is unlikely that you will master the basics so quickly as to require my intervention before a more advanced tutor is located."

14

KALI

"What can possibly be taking so long?" Wil demands, throwing down his cards. "It's been a week, and every day Bahir holds the throne makes the bastard more entrenched. You'd think His Majesty King Owain might condescend to see either us or his long-dead son before now."

"I cannot say," says Calvin from his now-usual place on the sturdiest of the chairs. "But perhaps Master Luca might spend the time in a more productive activity than teaching you how to cheat at cards, Your Highness."

Luca looks up. "I already tried dice and Wil is terrible. Cards are better."

"I do believe you missed the salient point," Calvin says dryly.

"The salient point is that we are trapped here." I set aside the light crystal Alexa is attempting to teach me to tune. So far, I've only managed to wrap my hand in darkness, the shadows creeping up to my elbow. "At least when we were in the forest, it felt like we were making progress." I scowl at the crystal

Rune located for me to practice on. He should have saved himself the trouble and brought me a rock instead. I've tried every exercise Alexa can think of, and still, the only thing I can make the light crystal do is hit Luca between the eyes at three paces.

Luca squints at my shadowed hand. "That's a neat trick, for dice especially. Is it difficult?"

I sever the flow of magic and my hand returns into view. "Unfortunately, yes." I sigh. "And until I discover a way to absorb additional magic, once my reserves are gone, they're gone. I wish I knew how Bahir does it."

"What else can you do so far?" asks Luca.

"Nothing," I groan. "I think absorbing light to create darkness is instinctual for me, but who knows what will happen if I replenish the magic from another breed of crystal. *If* I'm ever able to."

The tent flap opens, inviting in light, silence, and Rune. His silver-blond hair is brushed and tied back with a leather thong, leaving his square jaw exposed. He is dressed in full Everett uniform now: black pants, green jacket with golden buttons, a braid of gold ribbon encircling his shoulder. It looks good on him. Stars, everything looks good on him.

"Jasmine's fever broke," Rune says by way of greeting. "She should make a full recovery."

Alexa squeals, covering her mouth with her hands when Rune smiles at her. The smile fades as he turns to me and holds out a bundle. "It's for you."

I take the parcel tentatively, unwrapping the cloth to find an embroidered blue dress inside. The top is tight fitting but soft, with small gems sewn around the low neckline, while the skirt flares gently at the waist, whispering with the promise of easy movement and even riding. A pair of blue sapphire earrings, a matching necklace, and silver slippers complete the package. "It's . . . beautiful." I can't help the words. The truth. It is beautiful. Not fancy like the evening gowns Lady Lianna wore, but more of an everyday elegance designed to bring out the prettiest version of its wearer. My fingers brush the fabric as I look into Rune's face and catch a small blush rising beneath the skin. "Where did you find this?"

He shifts his weight. "There are some women in camp. Officers' wives . . . some others. I had one of the lieutenants ask around."

"And to what do I owe the pleasure?" I ask, my breath stilling.

Rune's eyes meet mine, so intense that my chest heats. Rune opens his mouth, but no words come and he closes it again. Shakes himself. "It is customary for women in Everett to dress like women," he says gruffly. "Your only clothes are of a guardsman trainee. This attire will be more appropriate."

A chill settles over us, and I gather up the garment. "Is there anyone specific we will be trying to avoid offending?" I ask, putting the dress into my bedroll. "Since I'm confined to the tent, it seems superfluous to actually change clothes. You can just tell the guards you saw me wearing whatever you think proper, and we'll leave it at that."

Rune tugs down on his uniform jacket, pulling his shoulders back as he surveys the room. I wonder what it's like to become a prince after years as a guard, whether he shifted into the role as smoothly as I turned into Lady Lianna, or whether each motion, each measured word, came at its own price.

Our eyes meet again, and in the split heartbeat before Rune catches himself, I have my answer.

He clears his throat. "We will be leaving tomorrow for River Manor."

"Is that what you call the palace?" Luca asks.

"No. River Manor is a family estate a few days' ride from the capital. My parents will meet us there."

"Hmm." Calvin makes a thoughtful sound in the back of his throat but asks nothing.

Rune draws a breath, raising his chin. "The men will travel by horseback and the ladies will ride in the wagon. Master Calvin, you may wish to ride in the wagon as well." Rune turns to me. "I apologize, Kalianna. The arrangement has no flexibility."

I raise a brow at him. "You want me to ride in the wagon with Alexa and Jasmine?"

"And Princess Raza, yes."

My mouth dries, my eyes widening as I find my voice. "Are you insane?" I say finally, with a calm that's absurd even to my ears. "If you are, I would truly prefer to know now."

Rune sighs. "This is not my ideal arrangement, but I've no alternative. I understand your fear, but I assure you that Raza—"

"My fear, Rune," I say, taking a step toward him until we are close enough for him to feel the heat of fury rolling off my body, "is that I will turn your little sister into dinner for any stray dogs we pass en route."

Rune's nostrils flare. "Then I'll be sure to clear the path of dogs to remove the temptation."

Wil clears his throat. "Why doesn't Kalianna ride a horse instead," he says. "She is a solid horseman, likely better than half the army, and she can dress as Kal if it will make the others feel better. Stars, Rune. She can take whatever horse you'd intended for me, and I'll keep Raza company in the wagon."

"That would be inappropriate in Everett, Prince William," Rune says without looking at him, before turning on his heels and striding to the exit. "I am sorry, but my kingdom's customs must be considered as much as yours."

A silence settles around us again, a twin to the one that heralded Rune's arrival. The heat in my veins turns to ice. "Wil," I say after a moment, turning to face him, "do you think you could call me Kali?"

"Kali?" says Wil.

I swallow. "It's what my family . . . what my sister calls me. I'd like my cousin to use it too."

A grin spreads over Wil's face. He's just opening his mouth, likely to try the name on for size, when Luca cuts in. "Kali," he says. "Yes. Easier than Kalianna and more appropriate than Kal. I'll take it."

I frown in confusion. "I was talking to Wil, actually. He's my cousin and . . . I mean, you aren't."

"How is that my fault?" Luca replies indignantly. He picks up the deck of cards. "Who is in for the next round?"

15

VIOLET

"*V*iolet, you need to get up." Leaf's gentle voice coaxed Violet's eyes open. "You need to get up," Leaf said again, this time urgently, her cool fingers running along Violet's skin.

Opening her eyes, Violet found Leaf sitting on the side of the bed. Despite her small size, Leaf was older—twenty—and she'd lost both a sister and a mother too. And a brother, in a way, given the stories Leaf told about Kal. The crippled girl was the strangest creature Violet had ever met, yet Leaf's very oddness completed Violet.

"Get up." Leaf poked Violet's ribs.

"Why bother?" Violet asked.

"Because," Leaf said dryly, "His Mighty Pompousness the Bishop of Creative Truths is bound to slink in here sooner rather than later, and it would be better if he did not find you abed. He has enough ideas of his own without you suggesting more."

"You really shouldn't call the Messenger that," said Violet, pushing herself up. Violet was tired. So very tired. No matter how much she slept. She *did* have to get up. That was the agreement the Messenger had made with her: Violet could have Leaf attend her in the palace, but only if Violet promised to get up and out of bed. Every day.

Leaf pulled a dress out of the closet. Something red and probably pretty, though Violet couldn't bring herself to care about the details. The chamber itself was an echo of Violet's old room; the damage from the fire she'd started had been repaired and repainted to suit the bishop's taste.

"I'm a whisperer. I think that alone has sunk me to the rock-bottom of his scale and dug a hole," said Leaf. "How are you feeling?"

Violet pulled on the offered dress. Unlike proper Children's attire, the dress was designed to be formfitting, but it hung like a rag off Violet's thin frame instead. Her body seemed to waste away more each night. How was she feeling? Like a doll being dressed into a queen.

"I'm afraid of my dreams," said Violet. "Each time I close my eyes, I—it doesn't matter. I mean, it's normal. A tithe to balance the sins of my birth parents' souls."

Leaf said nothing to that.

Violet swallowed. The problem wasn't the tithe; it was that Violet was just so tired of paying it. Comforting thoughts, like the peace her actions would bring to her mother's soul, were no longer enough. Violet missed sharing a room with her sisters, working shoulder to shoulder beside them, rising each day knowing she was making a difference in her kingdom. She never saw them nowadays. Zalia was busy as usual, and Dasha had discovered she was with child and had been instructed by Bahir to remain belowground and pray. Any deviation from that, Bahir warned, risked upsetting the Goddess.

"There are other ways to make an impact, you know," said Leaf, as if reading Violet's thoughts. "Maybe someone else can save souls for a bit, and you can focus on more important things."

"What could be more important?" asked Violet.

"Organizing socks," said Leaf.

A knock at the door prevented Violet's retort. The Messenger was here and the joy that his presence was supposed to herald was refusing to show itself.

Leaf kept her eyes lowered as she let the Messenger in and escorted him to the breakfast table, which a maid had already set for two while Violet slept. Eggs, fresh berries, tea. The sight of it turned Violet's stomach.

Bahir waited for Leaf to depart and for Violet to pull a chair out for him. "Are you feeling better?" he asked, laying a calloused hand on Violet's cheek before sitting down.

"I'm quite tired, Your Grace," Violet murmured. A headache was already pressing against the back of her head, and Violet longed for one of Leaf's droughts to soothe the pain.

"Poor lady." Bahir moved his hand from Violet's face to her shoulder. "Your body is treating you poorly these weeks, and it breaks my heart seeing you so."

Violet nodded and started toward the second chair, but the Messenger's hand on her shoulder tightened. "I held a vigil last night," he said, looking into her eyes. "I asked for the Goddess's guidance for how to ease this ailment that's befallen you. How to best fill you with her love."

Violet's chest tightened. "What guidance did she give you, Your Grace?" If there was another tithe, more that she had to do . . .

Bahir's thumb caressed Violet's skin. "We are healing Dansil, you and I," he murmured. "We are heralding the age of love and peace. The Goddess wants us to create life together."

"I don't understand."

Bahir smiled kindly. "A child. Healthy and happy, holy with the Messenger's seed. That is the gift the Goddess will grant you. And one you will in turn give your people."

Nausea shifted Violet's stomach. "I can't. I—"

"You would deny the Goddess's will?" Bahir demanded, pulling away his hand.

"I'm bleeding," Violet said quickly. "My cycle. I—" Acid rose in Violet's throat before she could finish the words, and she darted from the breakfast table to the chamber pot, heaving up her empty stomach. Violet was still bent over the porcelain when she heard Bahir moving about the suite, shifting things around, before the door opened and closed with his departure.

Stumbling back to the table for a sip of water, Violet found a rose waiting on the white tablecloth. Beside the flower, a note penned in Bahir's careful hand held three words.

Next week, then.

16

KALI

The three-day journey to River Manor is a haunting mirror of Leaf's and my carriage ride to Delta, not the least because it is Raza rather than Leaf sitting on the bench beside me. It takes me half a day just to push the thoughts of my sister from my mind enough to breathe normally. I've been doing well with not letting the reality of Leaf's absence conquer my mind, but my tether on that control is slipping more each day.

In place of Dansil's lush loneliness, Everett bursts with people. They are everywhere, crowding, bending against harsh winds, sucking air from each bit of space. Beggars shiver in the cold. Rich, bundled-up merchants squeeze into tiny tables at busy eateries. And stars, is it freezing. The farther we get from the Dansil border, the sharper the air's chill, cutting like a knife into my lungs. The last time it snowed in Dansil was before I was born. Here in Everett, we wake up each morning to frost-covered ground, and each night we hope no snowstorm will find our caravan.

If the people and the weather weren't enough to send my mind spinning, the parade of living crystals that streams by the carriage windows finishes the job. Staffs, jewelry, even building eaves all shine with living crystals. My own reserve of magic is gone, squandered in experiments and training and the occasional loss of control.

"Did you ever see Bahir siphon magic from a crystal?" I ask Alexa and Jasmine, the latter looking pale but way better than I last saw her. The girls have taken it upon themselves to try and tune Leaf's light and heat crystals into something I might draw magic from. As Rune is busy being everywhere I am not, the girls are my only authority on living crystals and their magic, my only tether to figuring out what being a mage entails. Everything that is squarely in Leaf's area of study. *Let me get Leaf back safe, and I promise never to ignore her magic lectures again,* I beg of the stars.

"No." Alexa fiddles with a lock of hair. "At first, we just tuned small light crystals, the little pebbles that Children sell. Then Bahir started us on more complex crystals and asked us to add triggers into the tunes so that the magic would activate on his command. The older whisperers worked on keeping the Eye of the Goddess shining bright. That was always the priority."

Right. I finger the living crystal in my hand, Alexa's latest attempt to tune it to my blood. Wrapping my hand around the crystal, I feel the stinging bees beneath my palm and imagine breathing them in. It doesn't work. My list of what *doesn't* work to replenish my magic reserves is quickly growing long enough to fill a scroll. Holding two crystals together doesn't work; concentrating really hard doesn't work. Punching a tree in frustration did work, but only to skin my knuckles.

I shake my head at a lantern hanging outside a boarding house, a light crystal instead of a flame flickering inside.

"What a waste." I shove myself away from the window, my palm catching on an errant nail head. I feel skin tearing. "A plain lantern would prove more efficient."

"The living crystal is a symbol of the inn's sophistication and luxury." Raza pulls her hood further over her mangled face. From another, the insight might have sounded helpful, but the princess has a knack for turning each breath into an insult.

I press my dress sleeve against the cut. "No wonder Everett is obsessed with the Sylthia mines. There can never be enough crystals if everyone needs to display one just to keep up their social status."

"Are you all right, Kal?" Jasmine inserts herself into the conversation before Raza can answer. As if any amount of peacemaking could bridge the gap between the princess and me.

"I'm fine," I sigh, holding up my hand. Stars, what I wouldn't give for some privacy. Or to be on horseback with the men instead of trapped here like cattle. The more I learn about Everett, the less I like it.

"Will you try tapping the crystal again, then?" Jasmine asks, holding the crystal out to me with her good arm. Attempt number one hundred forty-two. Give or take a few dozen.

"Waste of time." Raza crosses her legs. "A skilled whisperer can spoon-feed you magic through a healing crystal. And you can draw magic from stim crystals. A fact that, incidentally, you know thanks to me."

"You want credit for trying to kill me?" I take Jasmine's crystal, bracing myself for the stinging bees. "Stim crystals take months to make and they kill the crystals. Which I realize matters as little to you as—" I cut off with a gasp.

Jasmine and Alexa lean forward.

My hand is on fire, the magic scorching into the cut where

crystal meets blood. *Breathe,* I tell myself, struggling to absorb the magic instead of fighting it. *Breathe.* The crystal in my hand pulsates in time with my heartbeat. "The blood," I say when I can find my voice again. "The bleeding cut, that's what's different this time, what makes it work."

Jasmine's and Alexa's excited grins are almost as satisfying as Raza's deep scowl.

DESPITE THE LATE HOUR, I expect a flurry of activity to mark our arrival at River Manor, a colorful mansion with wide archways to welcome the breeze and plastered walls painted in pastel hues. It is a summer type of place, ill-suited for the day's chill. Finding only a small group of plainly dressed servants makes my skin crawl. Where is the livery, the pomp and circumstance, the courtiers who follow royalty? Even if this is meant as a calculated message to Wil, King Owain's personal stature—and that of his children—should warrant more crowds. A footman separates from the group, heading for our wagon. Raza's hands tighten on the seat's edge, her rapid breaths filling the small space.

I snap my wrist to drop a throwing knife into my palm, only to remember that my weapons are gone and the dress I'm wearing, however glorious, is not equipped to conceal vambraces anyway. "Who is he?" I demand of Raza.

"No one," the princess whispers. Her back shrinks against the seat.

I grab the front of her dress. "If you don't tell me who that man is right *now,* and explain exactly what threat he poses, I swear I will break you into tiny little pieces. Slowly. Understood?"

Raza shoves me away. "There is no threat," she hisses.

"Not to you." A trickle of blood spills from her lip where her teeth bit skin.

The man's hand reaches for the door and I growl.

"Oh, stand down, wildcat. He's just a footman." Raza finally meets my gaze. Silver lines her one remaining eye as she struggles to cover her face with her hood. "What do you think is wrong? Or have you gone blind?"

Oh, stars. Reaching past Raza and her vanity, I unlock the door myself.

"I know you want to kill me," Raza hisses at my back. "You think I'd mind? You think I *want* to face my parents as I am? You think there is anything for me in Everett now?"

"I don't think about you much, one way or the other," I say over my shoulder as the door opens and hands reach out to help me to the ground. I hold my skirts up as I descend, the hard-packed ground for once kind to my silver slippers. Wil finds me at once, the way he's done each evening when the caravan stopped for the night. Tonight, however, he offers me his arm.

I raise a brow and Wil blushes. "Seemed like a princely thing to do," he murmurs, his gaze pinned on the man and woman standing on the manor steps. "I think that's *them*."

I think Wil's right, though the king and queen are difficult to make out from this distance. Rune, on the other hand, is impossible to miss.

Still in his Everett uniform, his silhouette stands tall in the setting sun. The red sky beyond him frames the deadly grace of his movements, the gentle swing of his sword as he takes slow, deliberate steps toward the man and woman standing on the River Manor steps. The parents he left five years ago. The king and queen of a kingdom that called him a martyr.

Raza hurries to fall in step beside Rune.

They are ten paces from the steps when the man and woman turn their backs and walk inside.

"Might we escort Your Highness and his guests to their rooms?" A pair of servants has appeared beside Wil and me. "We've arranged a set of suites for the Dansil delegation."

My gaze skids between the servants and Rune, still standing tall before the now-empty steps. In spite of everything, I want to go to him, to put a hand on his shoulder. I'm no longer angry that the gesture would be unwelcome—just sad. I think that if there were no Prince Rune, if the man standing there were still Trace, things would be different between us.

Reality, however, is as inconsiderate as ever. He is Rune. And he is taking his rightful place as heir to Everett's throne.

Turning to the servants, I force a smile to my face. "A room sounds most lovely. Please, lead on."

The open-air corridors are as empty as the courtyard was, the servants few. A maid scurries about to place fresh-cut pine branches into vases plainly designed for summer flowers, and the fireplace in our sitting room has clearly been dormant for some time. "I'll have your dinner brought up," the maid says, showing herself out.

"No welcoming banquet, it seems," says Wil dryly, sitting down on a woven chair.

I sweep the rooms, a set of three bedrooms adjoining a common room that the six of us—the extent of the Dansil royal court, with the exception of Violet—now occupy. More woven furniture stares back at me, dusty with disuse and bearing thin flower-embroidered cushions. Plainly, we've not traveled to where King Owain happened to be when he received word of our presence, but rather to a place he specifically relocated to.

"Why are we here, do you think?" I ask, walking back into the common room.

Calvin moves closer to the fire, holding his weathered hands near the flames. "A more accurate question is: Why are we not elsewhere?" he says, rubbing his lip. "What does this River Manor offer that is not available at, say, the royal palace?"

A knock at the door heralds a servant with a tray of bread, cheese, fruit, and mulled wine. She sets it on the table and departs with a bow. Somewhere along the road to Everett, I painted our arrival as a loud, energetic achievement. A solution. I might as well have dreamt of touching clouds.

I sniff the bread. It isn't stale, but it isn't freshly baked either. As if it was brought to River Manor, not baked here. "Expediency and discretion would be my guess, Master Calvin."

The man nods. "Discretion about what?" he says, turning his palms to the flames. "That Prince William is seeking an audience?"

"I see no need for discretion on that account," says Wil.

A corner of Calvin's mouth twitches, pleased with the answer.

"You've worked this out, haven't you, Master Calvin?" I say, raising a brow. "You are asking questions to which you already know the answers."

He shrugs. "Perhaps. I do find it better to know the answer before the question. Professional habits are difficult to break."

BY THE NEXT MORNING, Wil has nearly worn a hole in the rug from pacing.

We eat breakfast in tense silence, and right when I'm worried that the prince might do something rash, there's a light knock on the door. Wil leaps up to answer it, finding a servant on the other side. "His Majesty King Owain requests the pleasure of your company, Prince William," the servant says.

My heart stutters. This is it, the capstone of the only chance we have. The hope that's kept us moving farther from Dansil every day will either flower or die in the next hour. I imagined that more flair would accompany this moment. A grand throne room, fancy clothes, grave-faced guards.

I imagined Rune standing beside us.

Wil holds his hand out to me. "If you will join me, cousin," he says formally for the servant's sake. "I feel that both representatives of Dansil royal blood should attend His Majesty." The servant, who knows protocol when he hears it, bows politely and motions for us to follow.

I memorize the layout of the manor as I walk beside Wil toward a downstairs room, each step filled with increasing tension. More woven chairs line our passage, and large windows with sheer curtains. Even with a fire burning in every hearth, the halls are too cold for comfort, especially in my low-necked dress.

The prince's pounding heart echoes through the hand I rest on his elbow. My own pulse keeps pace with his.

The servant stops before a half-closed door and opens it onto an empty sitting room. Warm air escapes from inside. "Please make yourselves comfortable." He makes no effort to hide just how little our comfort truly concerns him or anyone else. "His Majesty will join you shortly." The door shuts behind us with a sharp click.

17

KALI

*W*il spins around, whistling at the painted walls and carefully arranged furniture. As with the other rooms in River Manor, the style is lighter than the heavy chairs and velvet curtains of the Delta palace. The tall arched windows that bathe the room in bright sunlight also let in a cool draft. At least there is a fireplace—even if it's blazing up such a storm that, unlike every other place in the manor, the furious flames manage to make the room *too* warm.

I almost miss the slight movement at the far end of the room. My back stiffens, my eyes surveying the furniture anew. Wil takes a step toward me, his brows knitted in question. I shake my head and put my finger to my lips. Stepping slowly as to keep the floor from creaking, I move along the bookcases lining the wall. Stars, what I wouldn't give to have my knives back. The magic rumbles inside my chest.

Another breath of movement and a gentle whine of the floorboards. One person. Large. Standing in the small, blind space formed between the end of the bookshelf and the wall with the windows. My hand closes around a metal letter opener that I palm from a shelf. I pause, take a breath, spin around the bookcase—

And stop cold. "Why in the bloody hells are you hiding here?"

Rune flicks a brow at the letter opener in my fist. He is no longer wearing a uniform but is dressed in the Everett colors nonetheless, with forest-green pants and a heavy black coat that looks absurd in the warm room. "I am hardly hiding. It's the only decent piece of wall to lean against."

His eyes brush my silhouette, making me all too aware of the curves the dress accents perfectly.

I want to ask how his meeting with his parents went. I want him to ask after me. I cross my arms over my chest. "Don't let me intrude upon your resting spot, Your Highness. I'd hate for the boring business of Dansil's survival to be a bother."

"Kali—" Wil starts to say, but I hold up my hand.

Something about Rune's appearance bothers me. Something I can't quite put my finger on, like an itch deep between the shoulder blades. Perhaps it's his damn coat, or the too-rigid stance, or the look in his eye that is so void of emotion, even I cannot see beyond the mask. "What do you know?" I ask. "Has Owain made a decision already, without even hearing Wil out?"

"I do not know," Rune says evenly. The muscles beneath his clothes are coiled hard, even beyond the usual solidness that I remember excruciatingly well.

"You are his son. You've spent hours with him, and a week talking with his general and riding with his troops. You know *something.*" I let my arms drop, my voice doing the same. "I understand that you are the prince of Everett, Rune. I understand that you can't or won't have me in your life. Whether it's been a game all along—"

"Kal—"

I put up a hand, not letting him speak. Not yet. The words are too difficult to be voicing twice. "Or whether circumstances just changed," I continue, "it doesn't matter. I don't matter. What matters is that you've spent years protecting King Firehorn and his son, spent years smuggling whisperers from Bahir's grasp. You've put both your life and honor on the line. For the sake of all that effort, give us something to work with. Tell us what Owain is thinking, how we can best speak to him." My jaw clenches at Rune's silence, my blood simmering. "You know the importance of this meeting to us. Is helping us prepare for it so against Everett's best interests that you will not dare risk it?"

Rune's eyes flash. He tips his head down toward me, his perfect face and dark eyes a storm. "I don't know my father's mind about Dansil." He enunciates each word as one might to someone hard of hearing or simple of mind, and then he strides forward several steps, gaining a moment to nod his hello to Wil before the doors to the sitting room swing open again.

We all turn.

As silly as it is, my first thought upon seeing King Owain and Queen Maria up close is how much Rune takes after his parents. Owain and Rune are of a height, and the prince's jawbone is cut the same way as his father's. Queen Maria is plainly responsible for Rune's high cheekbones and Raza's ethereal beauty. Maria's eyes, a dazzling shade of emerald, echo in the pale green dress that flows behind her like the wings of a butterfly. Tall and lithe, she seems almost fragile next to Owain's steel eyes and Rune's deadly grace.

Owain halts a few steps into the room, far enough to force

us all to come to him. Rune is the last to move, but when he does, he strides all the way forward and drops to one knee before his father. I think of Lord Gapral, who wielded formality as a tool. Or a weapon. Neither good nor bad, just tactical.

Wil throws me a glance, as if asking my opinion on how to best greet the royal.

My gut tells me the glance is a mistake. Any sign of weakness is. Despite having all the power of Everett behind him, Owain has come to play hard. He'll exploit any possible advantage, even over a young prince finding his stride in a royal visit.

Then again, we've come as beggars. Perhaps it little matters after all.

Wil finally settles on a bow. I curtsy, staying with my skirts spread until the queen bids me to rise. Rune receives no such courtesy.

Wil clears his throat. "Thank you for granting me an audience on such . . . *short notice* hardly seems the right phrase." His boyish voice strives for gravity but surrenders to its casual cadence within a few words. He sticks his hands in his pockets.

"Shall we sit?" Owain says darkly, an ill-hidden attempt to minimize Wil's further assault on protocol.

Wil nods, steps back toward the sofa without looking, and trips on the carpet. Catching himself on the sofa's armrest, he controls his descent enough to land his backside on the seat instead of the floor. I let out a very slow breath.

"My condolences for the loss of your father, Prince William," King Owain says finally, apparently determined to battle impotence with formality. "How might I be of service to his son?" Wil waits until Maria and I have found our seats. When Rune stays kneeling, his black coat glistening in sunlit patches, Wil frowns questioningly at him. "Prince William,"

Owain enunciates sharply, "how might I be of service to the Dansil throne?"

Wil's attention snaps back to King Owain, and he raises his chin. A surge of energy rattles through me. This is it, the reason we've come, the last hope for Dansil. For Leaf.

Wil swallows. "Before my father's death, he and Envoy Jajack negotiated a peace agreement between our kingdoms. The official surrender of Sylthia lands to Everett and a peacekeeping force from your kingdom to support Dansil's throne. I come asking you for those troops."

Such plain, simple words. My breath stills as our future hangs silent in air crackling with judgment. Wil's hand grips his knee, his knuckles bloodless. My lungs burn. The *tick-tock* of a clock's pendulum is the only sign that time still moves. Slow. Heavy. Laden with the life and death of a kingdom.

Finally, slowly, King Owain tilts his head to the side. "I believe the situation in Dansil has somewhat altered since those negotiations took place."

My stomach sinks.

Wil's eyes dart to me, his head shaking in denial of the words, begging me to have heard something that he did not.

King Owain begins to rise.

"Yes, Your Majesty, it has changed." I hear my own voice before I make the decision to use it. I lean forward, my elbows digging into my thighs. Not a lady, but a scout. A very *good* scout. One determined to fight until the bitter end. "It's become worse for us all. Especially for Everett. Because the one poisonous dagger that the Dansil war has held against your kingdom's side—the terror mongers of Viva Sylthia—is now a country-backed, fully stocked force."

A tiny flinch of surprise flashes in Owain's dark eyes. He sits back down.

I press the assault. "Dansil has posed no true threat to

Everett for years, Your Majesty. It was Viva Sylthia's attacks that destroyed the living-crystal mines Everett had built up in Sylthia. The mines that Everett could competently protect are long dry, and the moderate-risk ones have crystals enough for perhaps a year. Likely less, given Everett's gluttony for living crystals. *That*, sir, is why you entered the ceasefire talks to begin with." I pause, meeting his eyes. "Bishop Bahir is the leader of Viva Sylthia. Is that who you want on the Dansil throne?"

Owain cocks a brow. "Fighting words, Lady Kalianna. But how am I to believe them? What evidence have you that the Goddess-loving Bishop is, in fact, the mastermind behind Viva's terror?"

"You have the evidence of my observations. I imagine my background as a scout is a poorly kept secret by now." I straighten my spine, my heart pounding, blood coursing fire through my veins. My ears ring with the music of war. "Additionally, our two young whisperers were Bahir's prisoners, and Questioner Calvin has interrogated a member of Bishop Bahir's scarlet guard—they can all offer their testimonies of the facts. Finally, there is the word of your own son, the prince of Everett, who has spent the past two years spying on the Dansil throne. Ask him."

Those last words spark a flash of pleasure in Owain's eyes. As if the trap he set had finally sprung. My chest tightens.

"Ah, yes, the boy." Owain looks over at Rune, who's still kneeling on the floor. "Lady Kalianna seems to believe you have something to say. Get up, then; take off that stifling coat and join the conversation."

Rune's face rises, his eyes blazing. "No."

"I insist." Owain's voice sends a shiver down my spine. "I'll have the fire stoked if you are cold. Unless you prefer that I—"

Rune comes smoothly to his feet and begins to work the buttons. Owain nods in pleased approval. Rune's dark eyes belie nothing, but the shine of dull fabric catches my attention again. Rune isn't cold; he's sweating. I can't help but draw a breath, curious as to whether Rune's familiar musky scent will cross the several paces of air between us. A stupid, odd curiosity in the middle of such a meeting. I look away quickly.

The scent does reach me. Not musk and sweat, but copper. My head snaps back to where Rune is folding his coat neatly over his arm. The back of his white linen shirt drips with bright red blood.

18

KALI

*N*ausea grips my throat, forging slowly into hatred. Owain knew—he *knew* what happened to Rune five years ago. What it did to him. And Owain had him whipped anyway. To make a point. To us, to Rune, to himself.

My mind jumps back to finding Rune hidden when we arrived. He wasn't trying to deceive us or eavesdrop, but to grasp a moment of privacy to collect himself. To button a heavy coat over a ruthlessly timed beating.

The only decent piece of wall to lean against, he said. He never said he was leaning against it with his back.

Owain pours himself a goblet of chilled wine. "Do not keep our guests in suspense, boy. Tell them what you were punished for."

My fingers curl into fists, my body going still as a poised viper. The magic stirs inside me, growling its rage and hate. It presses against me from the inside, pulsating with latent power.

Rune's eyes widen and focus on me, the first sign he gives of being aware of my presence. He holds my gaze now, his face a desperate warning to calm myself. "I received six lashes for failing to protect Princess Raza," he says evenly, the words uttered for his father, the tone kept gentle for me. *It's all right,* his tone lies. *I don't mind very much. Don't do something stupid. Not over this.* "Another dozen for impersonating the crown prince of Everett."

My jaw clenches, but I yank my magic back hard. Calvin's question comes back to me. Why *aren't* we at the royal palace?

Because with enough distance from the throne, this meeting can be made to never have happened.

King Owain straightens his tunic. "Prince Rune of Everett is dead," he says with a final, dismissive shrug. "But to your point, Lady Kalianna, I suspect your assessment of Bishop Bahir is accurate enough, though outdated." He smiles without humor. "Not that it greatly matters, but he did not take the throne directly following the coup. He actually placed Princess Violet atop it. If my scouts' reports are accurate, that is." Wil draws a hard breath. Owain smiles. "A minor detail, really. No one imagines Princess Violet to be anything but a puppet. Would Your Highness agree?"

Wil clenches his hands in his lap but nods.

"Well then, young prince," King Owain passes a goblet of wine to Wil and crosses his legs, "shall we discuss the final card you hold? Do not tell me the matter has failed to occur to you."

Wil scratches the back of his head. "Your pardon, sir, but there are so many things that have failed to occur to me in the past months that narrowing them down to find the one you wish to discuss is more challenging than it appears."

"Quite understandable." Owain leans forward, a predator moving in for the kill. "Given the trying times for our nations, Your Highness will surely forgive the direct words for the sake of clarity. Princess Raza was permitted to travel to Dansil for one reason only: to introduce King Firehorn to his future daughter-in-law."

For an instant, I'm certain I've misheard Owain, or at the very least misunderstood. But Wil's eyes are wide, and even Rune stiffens, which is a feat for someone already still as stone.

"I was unaware of this arrangement or negotiation," Wil says finally, wisely avoiding offering an explanation for his ignorance. Whether he knew nothing because Firehorn kept it secret or because Owain just made it up now is of little consequence.

"I'm quite aware that the bride's recent injury decreases her attractiveness, but Dansil's situation has changed as well." Owain smiles coolly. "Everett is not in the business of taking allies on charity, especially not the nation that murdered so many of my kingdom's sons. If you wish to secure Everett's assistance in reclaiming the throne, you shall bring something to the table more valuable than a sad handful of loyal servants."

"You want me to marry Princess Raza," Wil repeats dumbly.

No, everything inside me screams.

"Yes," says Owain. "Marry and crown as an equal, not just a consort. A dowry of Everett soldiers is a mighty offering. And we'll have the girl wear a veil as a matter of course. It might even become a new fashion amongst the women." He slaps his knees and rises. "Think on it."

The queen, silent all this time, comes to her feet as well. As Owain opens the door to exit, she leans down to kiss Rune's cheek. "I am pleased to see you well," she says gently. "For however long you might stay." Her gaze floats toward the door.

King Owain sighs, nods, and holds up five fingers before leaving without his wife. Five minutes.

Maria lays her slender fingers against Rune's face. "Do not think he made this decision lightly, Rune. Your father may sound like things matter little to him, but he has weighed all the options over the past weeks. He believes it for the best that you remain . . . in hiding."

A pleasanter way to say "dead." *Owain is a venom-filled monster*, I want to growl. I hold my tongue, though. Rune would little thank me for interfering now.

He looks up, meeting his mother's brilliant green eyes. "Raza has changed."

She sighs. "You must understand that you were the one raised for the throne since swaddle clothes, not her. To rise from a sibling's shadow to being heir to the throne has been a hard journey for her."

"She isn't a child, Mother."

"She's been the heir for less than five years. You must give her leeway."

Rune's face darkens, his eyes flashing with anger for the first time. "Leeway to do what, exactly? What she did in Camp—"

"I will hear no more." Maria draws herself to her full height. "Do not try to goad me into politics or playing favorites with my own children. I love you both, just the way you are." She gives him an indulgent smile. "Plus, when she is married, she will change once more. They always do." This last part, she directs at Wil and then, with a wink, she disappears out the door.

I stare after her.

Wil puts his undrunk goblet of wine on a side table and rises, running his hands through his hair. His bewildered eyes skip around the room. "I think I need a walk."

"Of course," I say, starting to rise.

Wil shakes his head. "Alone. I need to think. Please. Leave

me be." Turning on his heels, Wil strides from the room, leaving me, Rune, and silence.

The click of the door behind him shoots inexplicable panic through me. I press my back against the couch, my mouth suddenly dry, my palms sweaty.

"Are you all right?" Rune asks.

Of course I'm not all right. Nothing about this is all right. From the thrice-damned alliance that King Owain just proposed to the blood soaking Rune's shirt and the unjust fact that I feel more for the man standing before me than I was ever meant to.

I don't know what to say. Where to look. How to escape. "Are you?"

Rune shakes out his coat and sticks his arms into the sleeves, only the slowness of his movements belying any discomfort. "My father puts Everett first. As he should. He is a good ruler. That is more important than being a good father."

My head snaps to him, the last of the tethers holding my emotions at bay cracking like a dry twig. "He whipped you for being alive, Rune." Just saying the words sends molten iron through me. I want to burn Owain for hurting Rune—and throttle Rune for being hurt in the first place. It makes no sense, but nothing about Rune does.

He raises his chin. "He punished me for trying to strong-arm the public image of the throne. Tell me you don't understand. Look me in the eye and tell me your master would have done any different."

I rise, stepping toward him. A harsh, humorless laugh escapes my throat. "You want to know whether I understand? I do. Owain used you to send a message about his power. The same way he's used you for the past five years. As a message. A banner. An idea. You can feign blindness and justify his intent all you want, but I'm done with lies. Including lying to myself." I turn to the door. "Go to hell, and take your father with you."

"Wait."

I keep walking.

"Kali." His voice softens. "Please."

I hesitate. *Leave. Leave now,* a voice inside my head warns.

I turn.

"I've not lied to you," says Rune. "I just want that set straight before you leave."

My nostrils flare, my hands curling slowly into fists. "No, you're right. You kissed me, let me think you cared, let me . . . let me fall in love with you." I don't expect myself to say the words until they're out of my mouth, and I'm too angry to take them back. My pulse races, my breaths coming quick and shallow as if I'm readying for battle. The rest tumbles out so quickly that the sentences trip. "And then you told me you were leaving, and did—without ever looking back. The man who woke the morning after our last kiss had no interest in me, or room for me in his life. So no, you never lied, Rune. You were upfront and honest when you decided to trample on me."

Rune steps toward me, his eyes wide, his head shaking. "No. That's not—"

I step back. "Enough." My eyes sting with tears, which only makes me angrier. "You don't get to rewrite the past any more than you get to spin your father's horridness into wisdom." My chest heaves with hollow breaths, heart racing to outrun my own words. "What was I to you, *Your Highness*? A conquest? A distraction?"

"No." He lunges forward before I can move again and grabs both my shoulders. The strength of the warrior he is sings in every fiber. His face lowers to be level with mine. "You think I kept my distance because I *lost interest*? Stars. That would be like losing interest in air." He gives me a small shake.

"Kissing you was the most self-indulgent, selfish thing I could have done. You deserve better than an irrelevant symbol who couldn't even stop Luca's words when they cut you. I overstepped when I kissed you last time, and I've struggled to undo the damage every moment since." He releases me as if dropping a scalding kettle, and we stare at each other across a foot of sizzling air.

19

KALI

*M*y mind races. Hearing the words I've ached for day after day shatters my world all over again. I hate him for saying them, hate myself for wanting them. An offer of a drug just when the worst of the withdrawal has finally passed.

"I'm sorry." Rune steps away, showing empty palms. "You are right to despise me, Kal. Just do it for the right reasons."

I rub the heels of my hands over my eyes. I need a moment to think. Walking over to the closest armchair, I drop onto its cushion. My mind spins. Rune. Owain. Dansil. Leaf. My heart beats so hard, it eclipses the clock. The words I threw at Rune just moments ago, calling him nothing but a message, return to haunt me. There is no winning for us; the rules are rigged.

"Rigged?" Rune echoes, and I realize I said my last thought aloud. Which is just as well, because the embers smoldering in my blood billow into flames again.

"Rigged to tie your worth to your father's word. To make

me something that got swept along in the current. Someone else always pulling our strings. Why?"

Rune frowns. "I don't know," he says softly. "It just . . . is."

"Maybe it shouldn't be. Maybe we should stop fighting separate wars and make the rules our own." I capture his gaze. Hold it. Soften my voice. "Take off your shirt."

A step back. A nervous flicker in Rune's gray irises. "What? Why?"

"Because you were flogged, Rune. And you are bleeding. Would you be hiding those wounds if they'd come from a blade or a fist? Do you imagine your father doesn't know that?" I set out a chair beside a side table holding a pitcher of water. "He's using your ghosts to isolate you and to scare me and Wil into not daring to cross him. Let's not oblige."

His throat bobs.

"Take off your damn shirt, sit down, and trust me."

Rune's face clouds, tension painting every perfect line of his jaw. I pushed too hard, too fast. Wounds heal on their own schedule, not mine. Turning on his heels, Rune strides to the door, and my heart drops.

He grips the deadbolt and slides it home, then draws the shades over the open windows. That done, he draws a breath and removes his outer coat. His fingers slide to the buttons of his shirt, a slight tightening around his eyes betraying his pain.

I push his hands out of the way, undoing the buttons for him. The opened cloth reveals the hard muscles of his chest, the angled indent of his sternum, the sharp cut of tensed abdominals. I slide my thumbs beneath the shirt's lapels and ease it off his back. The cloth detaches with a wet whisper, the soaked fabric sliding to the floor. A drop of blood follows it down and splatters beside Rune's boots. He stands stone still, chest out, arms loose at his sides, head raised. The artery in his neck pulses so hard, I can see the skin twitch with each beat.

"If you were anyone else, I'd say you were frightened," I say with forced lightness.

He catches my hands. Our eyes lock. "I am."

I snort, but it's half-hearted. "I can't hurt you more than you already are."

His grip on my hands tightens. His face looms over mine, close enough to share breath. Raw tension vibrates beneath the taut, scarred skin of his chest. "Yes, you can."

"I won't." My voice barely breaks a whisper, the confession I uttered earlier haunting my memory. Maybe, in the heat of everything, he didn't hear my words. Didn't note what I said. Maybe it's not even true, for I know little of such things. I run my palm down the length of Rune's clavicle, the lightly trembling muscles beneath. *I won't hurt you, Rune. Can you trust me not to?*

He breathes hard and touches his forehead to mine.

An inferno lights inside me.

Its mate burns in Rune's dark gaze.

It would only take a small shift to press my mouth against his. I want to. I almost do. But before I can obey the impulse, I swallow, take a small step back. "Turn around and sit before you get blood on my clothes." My voice is raspy.

Reaching for the chair, Rune sets it before him with clean, deliberate motions. "Maybe there is a drop of poetic justice to it all," he says in a voice that tries too hard to sound offhanded. Straddling the chair, he crosses his arms over the back and rests his forehead on his arms. "In the woods with Wil, the day you arrived. When I—"

"No," I cut him off. "There is no justice in this. Understand?"

He turns his head to peer at me. "Yes, ma'am."

"Good." I repurpose the pitcher of drinking water into a washbasin and rip a hem off Rune's ruined shirt to use as a rag. My voice quiets. "That day—I should have taken the salve. I was lying when I told you I had my own."

"I know."

I shake my head, then take my first full look at his ravaged back and grow still. It must hurt like hells, but Rune only hisses when I press the damp cloth against the first of his wounds. I put my free hand on the front of his shoulder, and after a moment, his own hand comes up to cover mine and his breathing eases.

"Don't take my head off," Rune says tentatively after a minute, "but does the lack of bandages alter this plan at all?"

"What lack of bandages?" Striding over to the window, I rip a chunk of cloth from one of Owain's fine curtains and begin separating the fabric into strips.

20

KALI

I find Wil pacing the perimeter of River Manor and drag him back to our suite, where Rune has already assembled the others. Walking into the ambush, Wil's perplexed expression turns to bewilderment.

"I take it Rune and Kali are talking again?" he asks Luca by way of greeting.

Luca shrugs. "For about a quarter hour now."

I stumble, momentarily losing my train of thought to savor that fact. Yes. We are talking. And stars, I like it.

Wil and Luca exchange amused glances.

I hold up my hands. "Never mind that. And Rune's presence here has nothing to do with me. I mean, it does, but —" I close my eyes and pinch the bridge of my nose. "Wil, you can't marry Princess Raza."

He sighs, leaning against the wall and sliding down it to the floor. "Have we found an army somewhere that I don't know about?"

"Kali is right, Wil," Rune says evenly, catching my eyes at

the use of my name, asking permission. I nod and Rune smiles slightly before reclaiming his path of thought. "Even if Raza weren't poisonous, did you hear that line about crowning her an equal, not a consort? By Everett law, a father's power over his daughter never fully dissolves. Marry Raza and you are handing *King Owain* a seal of office. There are always strings attached to any aid my father offers. You have to have a stronghold of your own before engaging with him. On anything."

Luca raises a hand. "Just so I'm clear, which side is Rune on today? Or is he Trace again?"

"He's Rune," I tell Luca. "And we are on our own side. The side that is going to refuse to play by either Bahir's or Owain's playbook." I glance at Rune. He nods. I face the room again. "We need reinforcements. Powerful people who have little love for Bahir and no loyalty to Owain. Those would be the whisperers that the Order is enslaving. We return to Dansil, extract the whisperers, and then negotiate with Owain from a different vantage point. And," I hope my racing heart stays well away from my voice, "while we are in Dansil, Rune kills Bahir. Then Owain will have to acknowledge his existence, giving Rune influence over the treaty terms."

Silence.

Wil runs both hands through his hair. "You are crazy," he informs Rune and me finally. "And coming from me, that's an impressive distinction."

"Agreed on both counts," mutters Luca, his gaze shooting to Rune. "Stars, since when does he have more sense than you?"

"There are seven of us." Wil holds up seven fingers, as if to make sure that I fully comprehend the number. "*Seven.* And of that seven, two are young girls who've never held a weapon and one is an old man." He winces. "No disrespect, Calvin, but I imagine your talents are better suited for tasks other than rushing headlong onto a battlefield." Wil stares at the four fingers he has left and shakes the hand in the air. "By this count, I and my extensive military training are twenty-five percent of our invasion force."

Rune steps forward to stand by my shoulder. "We are seven," he agrees. "Two princes. A warrior. Two guides into the Order's underground passages. A man holding most of the kingdom's secrets. And a mage."

"Viva Sylthia terrorized two nations by using small units, not grand armies," I say, surveying the room to ensure that my point is hitting its mark. "Our power lies in our knowledge and agility. And in the fact that we'll be tapping people who want us to succeed. Jasmine and Alexa know the layout of the Order's headquarters. They can get us into the heart of the temple and then gather and calm the others. We come by night, extract the whisperers, and use my shadow to conceal the retreat. Come morning, panic sets in. And panicked soldiers make mistakes."

Rune nods. "One of those mistakes will leave Bahir open. One arrow and it is done."

"KALI." Rune closes the door behind him as he slips into our common room the following morning. My hands twitch at my sides, longing to touch him but thinking better of it. I'm unsure what we are to each other now—or what we *should* be until the fighting is over, until we reclaim the Dansil throne. Rune clasps his hands behind his back. "What have I missed this morning?"

"Calvin is working with the girls and his own memory to create detailed maps of the temple and abbey and draw up likely patrol schedules for the guards. Luca is sweet-talking the kitchen staff and will start pilfering supplies as soon as he can manage. Wil and I were going to go riding and get a routine established for when we leave. We'll also work out the staging route to get supplies and weapons out of the manor. How long do you think we have before the noose your father has around Wil's neck tightens beyond hope?" *How much longer can Dansil and Leaf wait?*

"I'd wager that Wil can play the indecisive prince with my father for another week, no more," Rune replies. "And we need to make the most of it. I would like to take your place riding with Wil. My father remembers me as a self-absorbed boy, and it will be simple enough to play into his expectations." Bitterness enters his voice, disappearing quickly behind a calm mask.

There is always a mask with Rune. Even when it's only the two of us.

"What of me?" I ask.

A small smile touches his face. "I have someone I'd like you to meet. Tell the servants you'd like to go in search of certain herbs in the forest and see if they can find you a pair of pants and a tunic to wear. It will be better if I'm not seen spending too much time looking after your wellbeing."

I lift a brow. "Scouts don't like surprises."

Rune gives me an infuriating snort. "Be in the woods on the backside of the stable by noon," he says, showing himself to the door before I can reply. "There's a large oak two hundred paces north. Make sure to sweep for a tail before going there."

A FEW HOURS LATER, I do as instructed, cursing Rune for mentioning nothing of the wasps that haunt this particular area of the forest. I'd have thought the bloody insects would be dead or sleeping in this weather, but apparently, Everett wasps have adapted to the chill and stand ready to harass visitors at a moment's notice.

I find Rune leaning against the massive oak when I arrive, a small satchel hanging over his shoulder and a hunched, vaguely human form standing beside him.

"Kalianna," he says with a formal bow to me, "allow me to introduce Mistress Bobenshish. Your new magic tutor."

The form moves to reveal a weathered face looking out from beneath a heavy cloak. One of Bobenshish's eyes is covered with a milky film, but the other, a brilliant sky blue, studies me intently. Motioning for Rune to give her the satchel, she dismisses the prince with a wave of a gnarled hand and lays out a ream of living crystals on the ground.

I follow Rune as he attempts to slink away, and I grab his arm. "Who is Mistress Bobenshish?" I murmur.

"A whisperer," Rune murmurs back. "One I trust to remain fully discrete, but mostly trust to not kill you. Good luck."

"Well then, little mage," Bobenshish calls disapprovingly, drawing me away from the retreating Rune. "Come here, drink up, and let's see what you can do."

The obvious answer is "not much," but I'm smart enough to keep my mouth shut and do as I'm told.

As many times as I'm told to do it.

We start by filling my reserves from light crystals that Bobenshish tunes expertly to my blood. I siphon the magic through a cut on my palm and practice concentrating and containing it. Unlike the oily magic of healing crystals, the magic from the light crystals is thin and pliable. It obeys my will easily and channels into a large shadow with great, but bearable, effort.

~

AFTER THREE DAYS of nonstop labor, I manage to channel a darkness ten paces across and hold it for a quarter hour. I spend the next six hours unable to lift my head. When I do, Bobenshish scowls at me. "Candy and child's games," she informs me.

"It worked," I mumble.

"You'd need to drink from more light crystals than you could possibly carry," she scoffs. "All for a quarter hour of brute force. In your fighting terms, you pulled back a bow. Once. Is there an army in any kingdom that would call that an *archer*?"

The next hours and days meld together as I siphon magic from every type of crystal we can find, from heat and healing crystals to the more exotic ones Bobenshish pulls out from somewhere. After some experimentation, the old witch concedes that light manipulation is most natural for me and redoubles her efforts on that front. She doesn't just want darkness—she wants light too, and she wants it shaped solidly. A dagger, a shield, a spear. Each of my waking moments is spent either in the midst of trying something impossible or shaking in exhaustion.

At the end of the week, I'm competent in bending shadow from light, I can summon the occasional dagger, and most importantly, I have stretched my capacity for holding and controlling magical reserves to what Bobenshish declares passable levels. I can even ingest magic from several crystal breeds at once, though the viscous healing magic is by far the most potent and difficult to control.

Bobenshish, however, informs Rune that I am more powerful than she likes and she would like for him to conjure up a couple of years for my training. Either that or we can just slit each other's throats now and save everyone the trip to Dansil.

Neither of Bobenshish's alternatives is an option, of course, and when the clock strikes three in the morning on the ninth day of our stay at River Manor, I gather up my things and slip out into the dark.

KALI

*W*e meet an hour before dawn at a trailhead half a league into the forest. The crisp night air prickles my eyes and mouth, and my breath mists in the full moon's soft light. I hear horses' neighs, heralding Wil and Rune's arrival. Luca, Calvin, and the girls are already here.

"No problem getting the horses, then?" I ask, petting a mare's soft flank. The thick, shiny winter coat feels wonderful beneath my palm.

"Turned them out in the far pasture last night." Wil checks their tack. "The hostlers won't know until the evening feeding. Our disappearance will be noted before the animals'."

Jasmine appears beside us, handing out dark tunics and trousers. Luca passes out weapons, inspecting each of us to ensure buckles are tight and metal bits are muted with strips of cloth. His hand hesitates as he reaches to test the strap at my chest. I kick him in the shin and he grins.

Rune presses a small bundle into my hands. "Not your real

ones," he whispers into my ear, his breath warm and tickling, "but perhaps they'll do."

I unwrap the gift and feel warmth of a different kind spread through me. A vambrace with throwing daggers. Looking up at Rune, I mouth my thanks. He nods, a few strands of silver hair peeking out from beneath a dark hat. Reaching up, I tuck away the stray hairs, letting my fingers feel the angled line of his jaw, brush along his high cheekbones. His skin has the clean roughness of a recent shave.

Rune catches my wrist, presses his cheek into my palm. One of the rare touches we've had all week. His chest expands and lowers with deep, even breaths. A mirror to mine.

"Are you two coming?" Wil says, letting his horse stick her large nose between Rune and me. I flush but Rune just chuckles softly before releasing me, the sound a soft rumble deep in his chest. I try to burn the perfection of this moment into my memory, a boon to hold on to through whatever comes.

Wil's mare huffs.

Right. Taking the offered reins from Wil's hand, I swing into my mare's saddle and nudge the horse to the head of the line, where Calvin already waits. The man has the maps memorized and will be our navigator while I take care of the forward safety. Reaching into the well of magic stirring gently beside my heart, I pull out a small strand of red-tinged light. The colored shade protects our night vision and illuminates our footing enough to protect the horses' legs, all without being the highly visible beacon that white light is.

Perhaps Mistress Bobenshish is more brilliant than I've given her credit for.

We travel all day, alternating between riding at a trot and dismounting to walk the horses. We don't dare push them harder. If they go lame, our five-day journey will take three times that. As the sun begins to snake toward the horizon, we come to the stream Calvin pegged as our camping spot for the night. "Not bad, your planning," I murmur to the old man, getting a hint of a smile in return.

"Wait until you see what the boys practiced while you played with magic," he says with a wink. "I think they could storm that abbey blindfolded and never run into a single wall."

We dismount in companionable silence, each member of the group eager to lend a helping hand. When Rune and I get up to do a security sweep and take watch, Luca rolls his eyes. Rune gives him a vulgar gesture that has Luca's laughter following us into the woods. My face heats and I burrow deeper into my cloak. "One good thing about returning to Dansil," I say, crossing my arms over my chest. "It's warmer."

Rune pulls off his coat and lays it over my shoulders. The thick cloth still traps his warmth and smells headily male.

I shake my head, but Rune touches a finger to my lips. His silver hair peeks out from under his wool hat to brush against his jaw. "I grew up in Everett. Even without the coat, I am better equipped for the weather. I would little put it past you to freeze to death before you realized you needed help."

"Your faith in my survival skills is overwhelming."

His brows rise together. "What survival skills, pray tell?"

I shove him. He shoves back, catching me before the back of my head can connect with a tree trunk. His eyes study my face, their dark irises kissed with a speckle of emerald. He swallows, as if just realizing his hands are still on me. The mist of his breath dances with mine. My heart gallops. I feel the reined-in strength of the arms supporting me, the warmth of Rune's palms blazing through layers of clothes. An errant snowflake lands on Rune's upper lip, and I am desperately curious as to what it would taste like. A tiny drop of ice on warm lips.

Clearly, Rune is right about my pitiful survival skills. A whole army could march on me right now and I wouldn't notice.

I clear my throat and find my footing. My legs regretfully take my full weight. The snowflake on Rune's lip melts and rolls down his mouth. I catch it with my finger.

Rune gasps lightly as my finger touches his lips. A rush of sudden desire heats the air between us. His eyes widen, his breath coming as quickly as mine does. His fingers slide up my neck, cradling the base of my head with a deadly strength tamed to a gentle touch. I inhale his scent. Familiar. Musky. Distinctly his.

I rise onto my toes, my mouth reaching toward his. I can already taste him. Exquisitely warm. Primal. My heart pounds.

Rune bends his head to let our lips complete their connection.

My heart halts in anticipation.

And sprints into a full gallop at the sudden pounding of approaching hoofbeats and a shrill yell. Rune and I spring apart.

A throwing dagger drops into my hand, Rune's sword already glistening in his. Our hobbled horses dance and whinny as they feel one of their own approaching. The horse is visible now, a single animal running too hard for the terrain. The rider, bundled in layers of wool, pulls up beside us with a hard jerk on the reins.

Rune grabs the bridle before the unhappy animal throws its burden to the ground. The sharp edge of his sword rests against the intruder's neck. "Who are you?" he demands. "And what are you doing here?"

"I wanted to ask the same of you." The rider pulls down her hood. "Don't just stand there, brother. Help me down off this beast."

22

KALI

"Stars, I'm weary." Raza sinks to the ground, rubbing the back of her neck. "Won't someone offer me water?"

"No," says Rune.

Wil, who's taken Raza's mount, swears loudly. "He's exhausted. And going lame."

Raza rolls her eyes. "He's a horse. There are others."

I swallow a growl, my body as frustrated with the interruption of its dance with Rune's as my mind is with the princess's presence. I take deep breaths and lean against a tree, struggling to calm my aroused senses before I do something to Rune's little sister that he cannot forgive.

Then again, he's glaring at Raza with enough fury to send any sane person groveling. "Why did you follow us?"

"I've come looking for my betrothed, of course," says Raza. "Now that I know what you and Father planned for me, that is."

A flicker of guilt shimmers through my wall of fury. I'd

spared not one thought for how Owain's plan would affect the second half of his proposed arrangement.

Rune, however, gives Raza no quarter. "Who saw you leave?" he demands.

"Everyone. I announced I was going for a ride around the estate and told each set of guards that the other was coming with me. They will be conferring with each other and searching the bridle paths for at least a day. Now, Prince William." Pulling herself straight, Raza strides to Wil and plucks the currycomb from his hand. "Let Rune care for the beast—he enjoys playing commoner. You've been so difficult to track down this past week. But now we have the chance to get to know each other."

"I think I know everything I need to know about you, Your Highness," Wil says.

"If we are to be married—"

"We aren't." Wil grabs a pick and tends to the horse's hooves, each movement taking him farther from the princess. Raza follows. Wil walks around to the other side of the horse. "I'm not marrying you, Raza." He bends around the horse's neck to get a direct line of sight to Rune. "Correction, the gelding isn't going lame, he *is* lame. Shouldn't be ridden."

"Then Raza will return on foot," Rune growls.

"No!" She spins around to face him. "Or I'll tell Father that your whore kidnapped my beloved Prince William at sword point and you went after them. When Father gets his hands on her, she'll miss Camp Vanguard."

Before I can utter a word in response, Raza is knocked to the ground, Rune's kneecap digging into her upper belly. The girl's good eye widens, her mouth working to draw denied breath. Rune's flushed face towers over her. Raza claws the dirt.

I'm moving before I know it, my fingers finding a tender

spot on Rune's neck and gripping hard. "Enough," I shout. "You've made your point. Are you twelve? Get the hells off your sister."

Rune twists to me, his nostrils flaring.

I lean my face closer to his, biting off my words. "You want to fight someone, fight me."

With a snarl, Rune pulls his knee from his sister's belly and storms away.

Raza, still on the ground, curls in on herself and sobs. And some stupid, irrational part of me actually feels bad for her. By my count, Raza has not a single person in the world who gives a damn about her existence, with the possible exception of Queen Maria, who is more puppet than person. Then again, with what Raza did to me at the camp, I'm not altogether surprised that no one wishes to share her company.

I find Rune at the edge of our camp, as far as one could get shy of being reckless. Something dark and wet glistens on his knuckles, and identical marks mar a nearby tree. Tension rolls off his body like a lightning storm.

"What the hells was that?" I demand, stalking up to him.

The warrior flexes his fingers. "I don't want her here."

"I don't want many things. What's your point?"

"You of all people will defend her?" Rune snaps.

I put my hands on my hips. Between finally getting to spend time with Rune and now Raza's appearance, this whole trek is becoming very complicated very quickly—and that's before even figuring our destination and mission into the equation. "Whoever that man was back there," I tell him, "the one who attacked a defenseless girl because she dared disobey his commands, is not the man I want at my side." Turning my back to him, I start toward camp.

"We are going into battle," Rune says behind me. "People follow orders or others die." When I turn my head, Rune is looking into the darkness. "We are here to save kingdoms," he says. "Raza is here for herself."

I don't slow down all the way to camp.

By the time the sun has set fully, Raza's sobs have become background noise, constant and familiar. She gets up neither to help with any of the camp chores nor to see after her own needs for food and shelter. She can lie there all night for all I care—it's tomorrow that frightens me. We can't send her back without her bringing the whole damn Everett army onto our tail, not to mention the logistics of how she would make it back to River Manor alone, without a rideable horse.

But keeping her with us . . . Stars.

"I don't see that we have much choice," says Wil quietly, coming up to sit beside me while Rune continues to take his frustration out on helpless trees. At least now he's channeling his emotions into chopping wood. Wil tries for a smile. "The silver lining is that if she is here, we can tie and gag her as needed. Who knows what kind of trouble she can cause out of sight."

My gaze rests on Rune, his muscles bunching and sliding with each hard chop of his ax. There is a thin sheen of sweat coating his skin and a distant set to his jaw. His body is here, but his mind is in some personal labyrinth of thought to which I'm not privy.

"Tell me more about Leaf." Wil pokes the fire.

I bite my lip. "Leaf . . . Leaf is a whisperer. By now, she might—"

"She's alive." Wil nods to punctuate his decree. "Until proven otherwise, Leaf is alive, and I want to know everything about her. I'm not losing another family member to my personal stupidity."

A lump forms in my throat and I suddenly understand Rune's need to chop wood. With nothing but the forest, the quiet, and the looming confrontation before us, escaping my thoughts is becoming more difficult by the second. Wil is right; Leaf is alive. And I know that, while we are all heading to Dansil to reclaim the throne, I'm heading there to pull Leaf from the flames. A rush of cold grips my spine. What if there's a choice? What if saving Dansil requires going left and saving Leaf calls for going right?

We are here to save kingdoms, Rune said. *Raza is here for herself.*

Am I all that different?

I realize that Wil is still waiting for me to speak, and so I start at the beginning, telling him about Lord Gapral's estate and Leaf's whispering and her brilliant mind until both our eyelids grow heavy and we make our way to sleep.

By the time I wake up to take my watch shift, Princess Raza has relocated closer to the fire. The hysterical paralysis must have lasted only until the rest of us disappeared from sight. Relieving Luca, I start my circuit to check the perimeter and horses.

All is quiet. Dark. Eerily peaceful.

When I return to the fire next, Raza is sitting up, her whole body shivering like a newborn foal's. I sigh and dig out a pair of crabapples that I picked on our trek yesterday. Sour but edible. Before I can reconsider, I toss the fruit at her feet.

Raza snatches up the apple and bites into it. Her face contorts. "You call this dinner?" She spits out the food. "It's disgusting."

I thought I was too hard on Rune, but maybe not. Maybe I'm just being too easy on the one-eyed monster. Spinning on my heels, I start my circuit again.

"I hate you," the princess murmurs hoarsely after me. "You ruined my life."

I stop, turn, and march myself right back to her. Crouching to Raza's level, I speak with cold, quiet cruelty.

"Stop kidding yourself, Raza. Rune left you before he ever met me."

Raza's emerald eye meets mine. "You think I don't know that?" she whispers softly before turning away and curling up into a ball.

THE FOLLOWING MORNING starts with Raza's detailed complaining. She doesn't see why she should be the one to ride double behind Alexa; why someone else can't collect the firewood; why Wil refuses to walk beside her. Even Calvin's patience stretches thin, though he channels the annoyance into fervently collecting willow bark and brewing a headache-easing tea when we stop to rest.

"This brew is revolting, Master Calvin," Rune says with respect as he sips the offering. "It is well made."

"Spoken like a healer," says Calvin with a small chuckle.

I bite my lip. Rune engaging with Calvin, the Dansil questioner, is a bridge I hadn't expected him to cross. Dansil's looming approach—and the gut-turning anxiety it heightens with each step—makes for new alliances, it seems. If Rune and Calvin can speak, maybe Rune and I are due for another conversation as well. Maybe more than a conversation.

Or maybe we should skip conversation altogether.

Getting off watch that night, I find myself heading for Rune's bedroll instead of mine, my heart hammering in my chest.

KALI

"Kali?" Rune bolts up from his bedroll as I kneel beside him. "What's wrong?"

My pulse racing, I lean toward him and brazenly press my mouth against his. "The lack of this," I say, pulling away to bring my lips close to his ear. "And more."

A quiet rumble vibrates Rune's chest, his hands on my shoulders, pushing me away. "Kali." His voice is heavy with warning. "Be careful. I've only so much willpower left."

"Willpower to do what?" I whisper, the calloused warmth of his hands on my arms so loud, I can barely hear his words.

"To stop myself from doing something that will get us both killed," Rune says. He growls softly, and in the next moment his arms shift, pushing me onto my back with him braced above me, his breath tickling my neck. "The things I want to do to you, Kali. To do with you . . . Stars." Rune turns his face, taking deep, lung-stretching breaths while my own come quick and shallow.

I put my hands on his chest, pleased to find that he is

sleeping without his shirt, and my palms press against smooth skin and sculpted muscle.

Rune grabs my wrists, pinning them to the ground. "This isn't the time for complications," he says, his voice raspy. "Not when we have a war to prepare for. When my father might find a way to execute me even if we are successful in reclaiming the Dansil throne. We need to keep our minds focused on . . ." He swallows. "On other things."

My chest tightens. "You don't want me?"

"I don't want a bigger target painted on your back than you already have," Rune says, his face leaning closer to mine. "I love you, Kali." My breath catches. Our faces are so close now that I can only see his eyes. "And for that, for you, I'm—"

"Then paint away," I whisper, cutting him off.

"What?"

"You said you love me." I lick my lips, my pulse now echoing through my whole body. "And I said, paint away. I don't care if you paint a target or a bouquet of flowers. Paint something, Rune, and we'll figure it all out later."

Rune draws a ragged breath, his whole body tensing before descending onto mine, his mouth claiming mine with a hunger my own body welcomes. No, not just welcomes—demands in flashes of ice and heat that start in my chest and work their way down to my thighs.

Rune pulls back and I moan softly in frustration.

"Quiet," Rune whispers into my ear before his lips find the space right behind my earlobe and kiss it softly.

I shiver.

Rune shifts his head, laying a trail of kisses down my jaw, the corner of my mouth, my neck. Each touch of his lips against my skin is like a tiny ember, a delicious little shock that stokes the flame steadily growing between my legs.

With my wrists still beneath Rune's iron hold, I arch my

hips into him without thought, feeling the hard bulge in the front of his breeches.

"Stars," Rune gasps, releasing his hold on me as he sits up and pants, his thighs now straddling my hips.

I buck in encouragement, my body pulsing with an excitement that my brain can't keep up with.

"Not here," Rune whispers between clenched teeth. "I will have you, Kali, but in a bed, in a room, in . . . in privacy." He rolls off of me, pulling me against him until my back is flush with his chest and his arms are wrapped around me like a cocoon. Rune's breaths are fast and hot against the back of my neck, but his solid body stills my squirming. "Sleep," he rasps. "Here with me. Sleep with me until morning, and stars save anyone who has a comment about it."

WE MAKE our final stop a half day's ride from Delta. A high-ground spot on the edge of a dense wood, with ample water and endless clusters of red and black berries growing on thorny branches. If all goes as planned, this is where we will lead the liberated whisperers. Hundreds of people and only the supplies of the land to survive by. At least Dansil's warm climate is on our side.

"And what then?" Raza asks, managing to stare down her nose at a whole expanse of land. "What are all these people going to do once you get them here? Has it occurred to you that they might prefer to go back to their families rather than fight in your war? Or is Rune going to hold the lot of them at sword point forever?"

"We'll work it out, Raza," says Wil over his shoulder, his voice filled with fatigue. "But let us tackle one impossible problem at a time, if you please."

She turns on him, like a predator smelling blood. "And what of your sister, Your Highness? Will you be rescuing Princess Violet as well?"

He turns away, but not quickly enough for the pain in his eyes to remain private. "Violet does not wish to be rescued."

"How do you know?" Raza presses, and Rune snarls a soft warning. "Are you even planning on asking her?"

"That's enough, Raza." Rune steps between her and Wil. The first words he's spoken to her directly since the day she arrived. "Violet is safer without association with us."

"Why should that be your choice?" Raza wheels on her brother. Her hand twitches to the patch covering what was once her eye before she storms away from us. "Why should everything always be *your* choice?"

AT FIRST LIGHT the next morning, I strap on my weapons and get ready to scout Delta in preparation for the assault. It feels good, putting my skills to work. Rune checks my weapons and gear with such careful attention that it borders on fussing. "We should go together," he says, for the tenth time.

"Remind me again where you learned to scout?" I say.

He glowers but steps back to let Luca come up to me. Luca hands me a bundle of cloth strips. "Trail markers. There will be a great deal of people on the way back, and we can't have it all rest on one of us being alive and in front." Luca gives me a grin. "Try and choose a path that a mere mortal like me can follow without breaking his neck, all right?"

I await further guidance, a reminder of what my chosen path should pass through and avoid, but Luca gives me the credit of trusting my judgment. His hand clasps my shoulder. A farewell and good luck and good hunting. I do the same. Luca's large shoulder is solid beneath my grasp.

Wil is next to wish me luck. The prince sticks his hands in his pockets and grins. "You get to have all the amusement. Quite unjust, I'll have you know."

"I promise to enjoy none of it," I tell him solemnly.

Wil laughs before the carefree mask falters. "Thank you, cousin," he says quietly. His voice falters. "If you do see Violet . . ."

I grip his forearm. "Then I shall watch her closely and tell you all I know."

Raza, standing closer than courtesy dictates, snorts demonstratively and turns away. "How fortunate for Violet," she calls, picking up a cloak and heading into the berry patch with a cooking pot.

My eyes follow Raza as she begins collecting berries, her dress and cloak catching on thorns more and more the farther she goes into the bushes. "I might be wrong, but it appears that your fiancée is in danger of doing something useful today," I murmur to Wil. He punches my shoulder.

I nod my final farewells, my eyes pausing on Rune's worried gaze.

"Good luck, scout," he says finally. "Be—"

"Safe, yes," I roll my eyes. "I know."

"Be thorough," he says.

KALI

*I*nstead of exiting the North Wood at the back of the palace, where we made our escape, I bend around Delta and walk into the town south of the palace, my face concealed in the deep shadow of my hood. The familiar streets where I once frantically searched for Wil; the Wandering Dog, where I recognized Samuels; the temple with its forever-glowing Eye of the Goddess—it all looks just as it did when I was here last, a lifetime ago.

The people, however, are different. No royal guardsmen in blue walk the streets, only the bishop's red-clad Holy Guard, though the latter are out in droves. Striding around like they rule the streets, the city. Because they do. The coup's bloodstains have been washed away, but the people's eyes are dull, resigned, or, at best, frightened. Not rebellious. Those who dared protest have long been silenced, it seems.

On street corners, Children of the Goddess proclaim the Messenger's glories, along with announcements of times for the next mass and places where those looking for work or housing may find aid. A young woman in scarlet skirts calls for girls past their first bleed to join her in a commune of family that the Messenger has opened. "Accept the Goddess's blessing and she will watch over you," the young woman promises. "And your children."

Stars, the bastard is promising children. For the past twenty years, two out of three babes in Dansil have been stillborn, and no blessing is changing that. But Bishop Bahir has always played well on desperation, hasn't he?

I'm about to turn off the street when a gaggle of children actually appears, skipping along as they sing a rhyme about Bahir's greatness, while a plump woman watches over the group.

I stop, stepping back before my gasp brings unwanted attention. Where the bloody hells did Bahir find the children? And where are the children's parents?

My gut tightens. I don't like this city.

But I'm not here to like it—I'm here to conquer it.

Putting an end to my sightseeing, I walk to the temple, merging with the crowds of devotees as I observe the layouts and guard shifts; so far, they match the plans Calvin and the girls drew up. Good. Getting eyes on the abbey behind the Temple of Dansil, where the whisperers are housed, is more difficult. The place is surrounded by a wall, and even scaling the trees and rooftops, I can see little inside beyond a covered courtyard. An aboveground dungeon.

This, too, matches the girls' description.

My heart beats hard as I stare at the limestone walls. If Leaf is alive, that is where Bahir's bastards would most likely have brought her. My muscles tighten with the need to scale the bloody wall this instant, but this isn't the time. Not yet. Shimmying down from the roof, I check my hood and meld with a stream of people, frowning at just how thick it has suddenly gotten. I'm just about to ask one of the hollow-eyed women where the bloody hells everyone is headed when a crier moving down the street answers the question for me.

"Princess Violet to address Dansil!" the red-clad man calls cheerily. "Come one, come all to the Delta Royal Palace! Princess Violet to address Dansil!"

Well, that's something. At least one of us will have news of their sibling today. I quicken my step, just an eager subject hurrying to hear the words of her betters, and join the crowds trampling the flowers in the main palace courtyard.

Trumpets call the masses outside the palace to attention, their familiar melody seconded by a sister call common to the Order's services. "Her Royal Highness Princess Violet of Dansil!" shouts the herald on the balcony. "And His Holy Grace the Messenger of the Goddess, Bishop Bahir." I listen to the applause, watch the faces. A mix of fear and devotion. Uncertainty.

The curtain opens. Violet, dressed in a flowing red gown that consumes her small fourteen-year-old frame, stands behind it. I weave my way closer until I can make out Violet's eyes, dull beside the brilliant rubies woven into her hair, staring blankly into the crowd. Her thin hands clutch her dress as she spreads the skirt to offer Bahir a curtsy.

The crowd claps harder.

Bahir smiles, brushing a finger along his goatee. The velvet robe hanging from his wide shoulders is bright and heavy with power.

Violet takes a step back and I see the outline of her ribs beneath the shiny cloth. Her lip paint, as bright as the day she stood on the path and revealed Wil's identity, now only underscores the sickly gray of her skin.

No one in the crowd seems to notice, however. Either

because they've not seen much of the princess before or because they little care.

An older girl in the uniform of a lady's maid appears at Violet's side and whispers something in the princess's ear that makes Violet smile. My breath halts, my eyes staring at the space the maid just occupied.

Violet looks to the side one more time, then raises her chin and steps forward. Bahir steps from the other side of the balcony at the same time and meets Violet in the center. Instead of a formal bow to the ruler of Dansil, he holds out his arm to the princess, who comes obediently to his side. The bishop smiles, wraps his arm around Violet's thin shoulders, and kisses the top of her head.

"I would like to thank the Goddess for watching over Dansil," Violet says in a voice that is loud, but holds nothing of the girl who caught Wil riding in the forest and tried to converse with the grownups at dinner. "And the Messenger, His Grace Bishop Bahir, who has led us to the prosperity we enjoy today. With their wisdom, Dansil is becoming a kingdom of peace and love, both for our bodies in this world and our souls in the next."

Violet goes to step back into the shadows but Bahir places a firm hand on her back and she changes direction, descending the stairs into the crowd instead, greeting her people.

I stare as old and young come up to Violet, some to say a few words, some to touch her hand. A girl in a stained and snarled cloak presses a small basket of berries into Violet's hand, speaking quickly. My instincts rally to pay attention, especially when I see the sudden small rise of Violet's chest, a flash of intensity in her face, both quickly covered. But I damn my instincts to hells and care about none of it.

I can't.

Everything that I am is still hanging on that balcony moments before the speech began. When a lady's maid came up to offer the princess words of encouragement. And then walked off, dragging a clubfoot behind her.

25

KALI

I don't tell the others about Leaf. Not because I don't trust them, but because I trust them too much to do the right thing. And the right thing means sticking to the plan to liberate the whisperers inside Bahir's compound. To bring hundreds of enslaved whisperers to safety.

Except Leaf isn't at the compound.

Sitting far from the cooking fire, I draw my knees up to my chest and watch the stars, as if the answer to my problem could be found among them.

"By this time tomorrow, we'll be inside Bahir's compound," Rune says behind me. He crouches, bringing his mouth to my ear so his words tickle. "And by this time two days later, the whisperers will be here."

I bristle and Rune leans away, frowning as he lays three light crystals on the mossy ground. Jasmine and Alexa have been tuning every living crystal we have to my blood so I can fill my reserves easily before morning. I am the mage. The great and powerful secret weapon against Bahir. So bloody secret that even I don't know what I can do, or how to do it very well.

"Something happened in Delta today, didn't it, Kali?" Rune says.

For a moment I contemplate telling him about Leaf after all, explaining how badly I want to go to the palace this very second to get her out. But I know him well enough to guess how that conversation will end: him admonishing me at best and putting me under guard at worst. He'll make it so I can blame him for Leaf's suffering instead of blaming myself.

"Nothing happened," I say shortly. Picking up one of the crystals, I make a *give me* motion toward Rune's boot. When Rune obediently produces his knife, I press the sharp edge into my palm. The bite is welcome. Burying my fist in a tree trunk would be welcome as well.

Rune takes the knife back. "I don't like that you must cut yourself."

I close my fingers around the crystal, letting the stinging bees seep into my blood. "Would you prefer I didn't gather all the magic I can just now?"

Rune catches my face, his strong fingers trapping my chin. "If you are trying to provoke a fight, you can just ask," he murmurs, the low, seductive voice biting my blood.

My face heats, my heart pounding as both magic and Rune's words reach inside me. My fingers tighten around the crystal so hard, my knuckles blanch. Do I want a fight? I bloody want something. And that something isn't gentle. My jaw clenches, my heart picking up speed.

"Kali?" Rune's musky scent fills my lungs.

I pull back.

His calloused fingers hold fast.

With the next breath, the control stretching inside me finally snaps. Fire floods my blood. Lashing forward, I shatter

Rune's grip on my chin and force my mouth over his. My free hand grabs the back of Rune's neck, my nails raking his skin. My pulse races, my lips pressing harder.

My kiss doesn't ask. It takes.

Rune is still for a moment, then jerks forward, flattening me onto my back with a force to match my own. The hard ground hits the back of my head, a knobby root driving itself into my side. I don't care about the pain, only about Rune's body following me down, his mouth claiming mine even as his hands pin my shoulders to the ground.

My heart hammers harder, each beat so saturated that I feel it through my core. That it hurts. My nails dig deeper into Rune, demanding more.

Rune pulls away suddenly, his chest heaving as he looks down at me. A growl escapes his throat, his whole body a ball of hard muscle fighting against itself. "Kali," he breathes.

I wrap my legs around Rune's waist and jerk him forward until his upper body falls atop mine again, his mouth a breath away from my face.

"No." Rune pushes away, managing to get to his feet while I remain on the ground, panting into the cold, hard earth. "This isn't you, Kali," he says, each word strained. His fingers flex and open at his sides. "This isn't what our first time will be."

"Why the bloody hells not?" I shout to be heard over my throbbing need.

"Because when I take you, it will be for the right reason. Love—not distraction from whatever has you on edge."

I say nothing, my body shaking.

"What happened in Delta today?" Rune asks, crouching again but this time keeping his distance. "Let me in, Kali. Whatever's happened, we'll face it together."

"Nothing!" I shake my head, my body still trembling.

"Nothing." I climb to my feet, my palm shooting forward to halt Rune's approach. "Don't. If you won't do anything, then let me be. A scout prepares alone."

∼

"I still dislike Wil going with us." I frown at the prince as we strap our gear into place, and I ignore Rune's eyes altogether. My face flames with the memory of last night, not that I can do anything about it now.

Leaf's image burns my mind, and it's a fight to press it down. But I have to. I worked it out while I didn't sleep last night. Right now, I have to be present for the current mission, but once the whisperers are free . . . I tuck that promise away too. Since my companions will have no say in the matter, they need not carry this weight on their shoulders. "The Order is well inside Delta, and he's too bloody recognizable," I continue.

Wil looks down at himself. Black trousers and shirt, soot concealing his skin, a dark hat, and a decent arsenal of weapons hugs his elegant frame. "I can barely recognize myself."

"If you are caught—"

"If any of us are caught, the fate will be the same." Rune's voice is justly unhappy with me.

Still unable to meet Rune's eyes, I shift my weight, forcing my attention to the immediate difficulties. This operation was so much simpler before I glimpsed Leaf behind the curtain of the palace balcony—before I started wondering whether my own plan might be putting her in danger. Some fool's bargain inside me longs to keep Wil safe as an offering to the stars for Leaf's life. Taking a deep breath, I shove away that thought as well and reach for my magic instead. "Let's move out, then."

I take the lead as our group flows like a river into the trees. Once I get us through the thickest part of the forest, I yield the front position to Rune, who leads us the rest of the way through the old routes he put in place for the Order's runaways. Within an hour, the massive abbey looms before us, cold, windowless, and unwelcoming.

This is it. After we enter this building, we will either leave it with a force of whisperers great enough to make a difference in reclaiming Delta, or we will leave it in body bags. My heart slows, readying for the next move, each too-loud step of my untrained companions grating to my ears.

The shadow of my magic covers us as we crouch by the side entrance, listening to the pair of guards by the door cough and fart. The bell tolls the time, confirming that we've arrived an hour into the current shift. Relief is not due for another three hours, and I hope there are no overachievers among Bahir's men today.

Rune squeezes my shoulder to signal his readiness. Even if my companions hadn't spent a week rehearsing this while I learned the basics of magic, storming an abbey is a soldier's job, not a scout's. Rune will hold command from now on. My shadows and I are but a tool in his arsenal. A very powerful tool.

I pass Rune's squeeze on to Wil. It travels like that down the line, through Jasmine and Alexa and finally to Luca in the rear. He sends it back. The moment my hand touches Rune's shoulder again, he tosses the stone in his hand against the abbey wall.

The guards twitch. Turn to the noise. One walks toward us. The lantern he holds swings back and forth in his hand, the light a pale yellow. *Three. Two. One.* I count the guard's steps toward my shadow. *Now.*

I tap into my magic and use it to divert the lantern's light. Blackness engulfs both men.

The guard closer to us curses and stops to fiddle with a lamp that isn't really broken. "What's going on?" his partner calls into the dark. I feel Rune move, trusting his body to my darkness as he takes the guard down. The scuffle is over before it starts, a bloody gurgle confirming the guards no longer pose a risk. My heart beats hard against my ribs as I hold my position and our shadow, listening to Rune strip the sentries of their weapons and keys. When he returns to squeeze my shoulder, I smell the copper of the guards' blood on his hands.

It has begun.

KALI

I let a small red bit of light illuminate Rune's hands as he slides the guard's key into the door. The small click and creak of hinges takes my breath. We file inside, Rune taking the vanguard post again and Luca falling back to rear guard. The girls' ragged breaths sound behind me. They're terrified, but they follow.

Holding my throwing knives at the ready, I visualize the maps that Calvin and the girls put together. This corridor runs west to east, heading toward the guard barracks and workrooms. The whisperer dormitories are one level up.

"Kali," Rune whispers from the darkness, his voice carrying bare inches. "Release the shadow and save your strength."

"I'm fine."

The next breath I take is cut short by a male body pinning me against the stone. Rune's scent fills my nose as he leans so close to me that his breath tickles my cheek.

"Orders," he breathes, almost beyond hearing. "A scout

works alone, but a soldier does not. This succeeds only if you follow orders. Understand?"

I glare toward where I know his eyes must be, my pride coursing like fire through my veins. Rune's heart beats hard enough that I feel it ram his ribs. His lips brush my ear, his voice as unforgiving as the warrior himself. "If something has happened, if you cannot do this, I need to know *now*."

Not a threat, not really. A commander reassessing his forces. Deciding which he can do without. Which he *must* do without. The back of my head stings where it scraped stone. As do my eyes. I hate him for being right, but I release my magic. The natural darkness is thinner than my shadow but dark enough.

"Get in the back of the line," he orders, the tension in his muscles daring me to protest the punishment.

I turn my back to move down and feel the feather-soft touch of Rune's fingers between my shoulder blades. A tiny ember of comfort to dull the blow. I don't want it. Finding Luca, I murmur a few words that have him moving up to take the number-two slot in the stack while I fall in behind Wil and the girls. The stack moves forward. A silent single file, each person running one hand along the stone wall. Our steps and light breathing are the only sounds.

The line stops sooner than my step count tells me we should. A signal of squeezes from the front has us flattening against the wall. Closing my eyes, I try to discard the noise of the others' rapid breaths and locate the source of whatever has caught Rune's attention.

There. A distant scraping of boots. A voice calling to another. Someone is awake but not moving toward us. Not yet.

We start out again.

Another hesitation. Another signal. The step count puts us near the first of the barracks doors, but where there should be only the silence of sleeping guardsmen, there is cursing coming from down the hall instead. Two voices. A pair of guards heading to their beds. A signal from Rune is passed back to me, and I pull a shadow over us. My sword whispers from its sheath as we push back to clear the way to the barracks door. Alexa trips, gasping softly as I catch her arm.

One of the guards hesitates, the sound of his boots deafeningly close.

I feel the group's collective resolve, ready to kill if the guards decide to explore the noise. A pair of lives to be forfeited because a young girl tripped in the darkness. *It would be their own fault,* I insist, arguing with my conscience. *Sloppy security.* No one dared raise a hand against Bahir's sacred grounds when Firehorn held the throne, and now, with Bahir holding the whole city, the guards are bloody confident that their job ends at keeping frightened and unarmed whisperers from escaping. *If the guards die, it will be their own fault.*

After a moment, the guards choose their beds over their duty and walk into their sleeping quarters. Relief floods me. Rune signals and I release the shadow, sheathing my sword.

When we reach their quarters, Rune jams a small wedge of wood under the doorframe. Our first claim to control of the abbey's passages. Three more doors get the same treatment. I hope to the stars that none of the guards inside will decide to leave their cots.

With the corridor secured, we turn to finding someone with keys to the acolyte rooms upstairs. Rune motions me up beside him, and I pull the veil of darkness around us again as we creep toward the enclosed courtyard. The walkway running along the yard's perimeter is empty, yellow lanterns casting long shadows onto pale stone, but the distant sounds of a living abbey trickle down its spine. Someone will walk by.

Soon. Alexa and Jasmine come up to join us, trembling. It's up to them to recognize a key bearer.

"No one can see us," I whisper into their ears. "We are darkness."

Despite the sounds of life, it's ages before the first person walks by. The girls shake their heads. We wait again. Then again. Again. Again. I hold the shadow, our cloak of invisibility. I feel the others shift their feet, hear their unspoken questions. *Are you sure? Take another look. Maybe this one has keys?* It's all taking too long. Any heartbeat now, the soldiers will discover their doors jammed closed and raise a fuss.

"Her." Alexa clenches my hand so hard, I feel her nails break my skin. "Blond hair, walking across the courtyard now."

Rune stands as still as my shadow. My stomach tightens. The mark approaching us is but a girl herself. Sixteen, if that. Skinny. Unarmed. "Are you sure?"

"Yes," says Jasmine in a voice so cold it sends shivers through me. "Her name is Zalia. She has keys. Kill her for them."

Ice coats my blood, my face jerking to Rune. A young girl. Zalia is just a naive young girl. Whatever she's done to earn Jasmine's hatred, she couldn't have understood the full impact of it. She's a pawn of Bahir's, like so many others.

As if feeling my stare, Rune shifts toward me. "It's my call," he says quietly. A commander on a battlefield, in charge and responsible—for both the mission's success and the costs that will haunt future nightmares. The cost of getting to give the orders. My hands tremble as I count the steps until Zalia reaches the juncture where we stand. Fifteen paces left. Ten. Five.

Zalia turns down a side passage just before reaching our snare. I release a breath, my body sagging in on itself in relief.

What in the stars' name will we do for the sake of the greater good before the night ends? How many innocents will our crusade to save Dansil sacrifice?

"Zalia!" Jasmine rips away from the wall and sprints into the light of the courtyard. I curse. Rune snorts. Jasmine spins around herself, studying the walls as if she's never laid eyes on the stone before. Her small body, lithe as a dancer's, spins around a pillar.

"Jasmine?" the girl's voice calls warily. Zalia. The girl's name is Zalia. And she has no idea what's happening. "What in the name of the Goddess are you doing here?"

Jasmine shrugs. Spins around again. Waits. A predator playing prey. Zalia moves toward her. Another girl follows in Zalia's wake. As the two step into the lantern light, I catch the other girl's swayed back and swollen belly, not yet heavy but clearly there. A child. The girl is with child.

No. No. NO.

"Not your call," Rune says softly into my ear, his hand squeezing my shoulder. As much comfort as he can offer just now.

"Stay with me," the pregnant girl begs of Zalia. "Please."

"Stop it, Dasha," Zalia chides. "I need to see to this acolyte. The Messenger's work takes priority in our hearts. You know that."

Go back, I yell silently to Zalia's companion. *Go back. Hide. Run.* My hands tremble at my sides and I know it's a good thing indeed that I'm not in charge of this mission. Jasmine takes a step toward us, leading Zalia and her friend right toward our blades. I feel Luca move up to stand beside Rune and hear him take a sharp breath as he gets a full view of the girls.

"Stars," Luca breathes. "Is she—"

"Quiet," Rune orders. Cold. Unyielding. Nothing like the

mess I am. "Prepare the shadow, Kal. *Now.*"

I do it. Obeying Rune's order, I throw the shadow wide enough to cover the girls, flinching at their sudden muffled screams as Luca and Rune clamp their hands over the girls' faces. I press myself against the wall, drinking in the coolness to calm my nerves.

"Stairs," Rune says, his order coming as smooth and calm as ever. "Move."

I let the shadow dissolve enough to keep us from breaking our necks and nearly sob with relief when I find the captives gagged, not silenced forever. It could have gone either way, I know. I saw the resolve in Rune's face to do what had to be done to save all the others. Wil's eyes are wide, his gaze pinned on the pregnant Dasha as we move up the stairs and slide the key into the first of the acolyte dormitory doors. Waiting for no one, Jasmine slips inside.

The answering commotion is instantaneous and deafening. Screams, questions, yelps, as body after body floods out of the room and into the corridor. Pushing. Tripping. Falling. Grabbing for clothes or friends or shoes. Rune's orders of silence, given with enough cold command to still any warrior in his tracks, fall on deaf ears among these panicked young women. So many of them. Stars. Dozens in this one room alone. All making enough racket that the abbey will turn into a tomb for us all.

My magic stirs inside me. Without daring a heartbeat more thought, I throw myself into the noise, pretending it's light that I can absorb and bend, substituting with power what I lack in skill.

The world quiets. Sways.

"Kal," Rune's lips scream without sound. I blink at him. The magic pounds my insides. I drop to one knee. Rune drops beside me, his sword out and ready. Luca and Wil move down the corridor, opening door after door. More people come, girls and boys, young men and women. And more still.

The noise I'm absorbing booms inside my head, threatening to split my skull. I grab my temples with my palms, rocking myself. My eyes shut. The yelling, the scraping of feet on stone, the echoes of sound along stone walls, all assault me like vipers.

I feel a wet warmth inside my ear and realize it's blood. I open my eyes to a shaking world. Except the world isn't the one shaking—I am. Rune pries my hands from my head. *Stop*, his lips command. *Stop. You did enough.*

My magic's dam crashes. The hysterical sobs of the pregnant girl as she is herded along with the liberated whisperers is the first sound I hear. Crying for her baby's life.

"Is it my imagination, or does the girl with child look familiar?" Luca asks, falling back to where Rune and I cover the rear of the escaping whisperers. "I'm certain I've never seen her before, but her face . . ."

"Her brother was a guardsman trainee," Rune answers curtly. "Novan."

My breath catches. "You told me—"

"I told you the Holy Guard killed him over a girl," Rune says. "I never specified the circumstances."

"We'll need to tell Wil," says Luca, frowning down the corridor.

The sleeping guards inside the barracks have awoken and now bang on their jammed doors like crazed apes. A few more minutes and they'll break through. Four more roses, who must have been on duty at another part of the compound, now rush at us, their swords drawn.

"Luca, go on with the whisperers," Rune says, readying his blade. "Kali and I will hold these guards off until you have everyone out."

Luca nods and pushes past us, leaving Rune and me shoulder to shoulder against the coming patrol. My heart quickens then slows as the first of the men reaches us and Rune cuts him down with a mighty slash. I raise my sword in time to block a blow aimed for my head, the force of the attack slipping down my angled blade.

The rose swings again, this time a slice across my abdomen that I narrowly avoid by leaping back. My feet land on the stone, springing right back into the fight while the rose's own momentum makes him spin off balance. I watch his body. His hips. His eyes suddenly widening in bewildered recognition as he gets a good look at me and blanches.

"Kal is dead!" he screams.

"No, that would be you." I lunge, my blade piercing flesh deep enough to make my words true.

Rune shoots me a smile. Of course, he dispatched three men to my one, but we can count that up later.

Or not. The energy of the fight still pumping through me fades as I follow Rune out the door and bar it from the outside. Fresh night wind kisses my face, ruffling my hair and clothes. Led by Luca, Wil, and the girls, the whisperers are moving away from the abbey and toward the North Wood already, many picking up sticks and rocks to use as weapons as they go.

"That went better than expected," Rune says, letting out a long breath.

I don't answer. Rune's mission did go better than we could have hoped, but mine has yet to start.

Rune looks at me and frowns, his eyes growing increasingly wary. "It's time to leave."

"I know," I say softly. "But I can't go with you." Turning my back to Rune, I sprint into the darkness.

27

VIOLET

*V*iolet sat awake in her bed, listening to Leaf's soft snores. Leaf, who was really Violet's cousin. Leaf, whose absurd words and evening stories had kept Violet going, even when her own thoughts threatened to drown her. Who thought old texts and unanswerable questions and strange equations were going to change something.

Maybe if Violet had had Leaf for a sister, things would have been different. But that's not how everything had turned out.

Reaching under her pillow, Violet withdrew the small berry-stained note the girl in the courtyard had pressed into Violet's hand. Her heart quickened as she unfolded the parchment again and fingered the ribbon of cloth tucked inside, the moment coming back to her in vivid detail.

"From one prince's sister to another," the girl had whispered in a voice Violet knew well. Princess Raza.

"What is it?" Violet asked.

"Information. Because our brothers and fathers shouldn't keep us in the dark."

Confusion washed over Violet, but Raza was already bowing and moving away.

"I was given no choices of my own," Raza said. "But now, you are."

Raza was gone before Violet could ask more, but the note and cloth remained. Violet reread the words.

Your brother tries to kill Bahir tonight. The markers will lead you to his camp.

Stars. Wil. Violet didn't let herself feel the impact of that thought. She was getting skilled at not feeling. Sitting up, Violet let her bare feet touch the cold stone floor. It was just a note. She could throw it into the fire and leave the fate of both Bishop Bahir and Prince William in the Goddess's hands.

Or she could warn Bahir.

Violet's hand dropped to her belly, which may or may not hold a child. Her next gift to her people. She knew she should be content with such a future, but she wasn't. And perhaps, just perhaps, the Goddess knew that too. Perhaps today had been a codex meant just for Violet.

Violet's heart pounded, her palms growing slick with sweat despite the cool room. After a lifetime of wishing she had a say in decisions, she now faced the single greatest choice of her life.

Violet rose quietly and pulled on a pious red skirt and tunic. Padding over to the small chest where Leaf stored salves and tinctures, Violet withdrew a vial and tucked it into her pocket. She jotted a quick note to leave in the vial's place and headed to the door.

"Are you all right?" Leaf's sleepy voice startled a gasp from Violet.

Violet panted, a hand to her breast. "I am," she said once she'd found her voice. "Go back to sleep."

Leaf murmured something before resuming her slumber, and to Violet's infinite surprise, she realized that she *was* all right. Relieved. Even happy. Because tonight the Goddess had given her a chance to save her kingdom and her soul.

~

Kali

WRAPPING MYSELF IN DARKNESS, I stick to the woods as I make my way to the palace and slip underground through one of the catacomb exits. Between the night's natural dimness, my own summoned shadow and training, and my extensive familiarity with all the passageways, avoiding the night-shift guards is easy enough.

Finding Leaf is another matter. The knowledge that she is somewhere within these walls burns like acid in my veins. *Where? Where? Where?* The question rings in my mind as I slide along the dark corridors, the palace a sleeping ghost of its once-vibrant self. Scant yellow light bleeds from the occasional candle set into the wall, and the distant echoes of closing doors and feet scraping on stone are all the more deafening for being rare. I check our old rooms, the servants' hall, the privy, my blood rushing faster each time I come up emptyhanded.

Finally, the only place left to try is also one of the few guarded rooms in the whole palace—Princess Violet's suite. A lantern outside her door lights the approach, illuminating the two wide-awake men standing vigil.

Bracing myself, I slide into shadow, tucking my body into a

corner just away from Violet's door. A throwing knife slides into my palm, my heart thumping hard. Taking long, slow breaths, I memorize the guards' exact positions. A moment of surprise is all I'll have before they move, and I'll be as blind as they are. Another breath and my body coils, preparing to spring.

Now.

I lash out with my shadow, flooding the several paces between the guards and me with darkness. Sprinting forward, I pull the noise in toward me as well. Black silence descends on us like a shawl. I keep moving, keep dancing the steps I planned back in my corner.

My left hand finds the first guard's hair. I grab, aim with my mind, and strike the hilt of the dagger into the man's temple.

He falls, his weight crushing me before I slither to the side. His unconscious body makes no noise as it strikes the ground.

My head pulses. I spin toward where the other guard should be and feel the slight shift of air that betrays motion. I'm blind. Deaf. I know neither whether my opponent has drawn his blade, nor whether he is plunging it toward me this very heartbeat.

I crouch low to the ground. Straightening my leg, I sweep it around me in a circle. My ankle connects with a shin but the angle is wrong, and my prey fails to budge. But now we both know where the other is. My breath leaps away as a heavy boot strikes my belly. I grit my teeth and lunge at where the kicker's legs must be.

My arms clamp around the man's knees, my shoulder pressing into his thigh. I pivot to the side and tighten my arms, collapsing his legs altogether. A shove of my shoulder has the man falling to the side with a thud that I feel but don't hear. I follow him down, scrambling along his body toward his head. I feel the sharp, shallow bite of his sword along my ribs before the hilt of my dagger connects with his temple. The body stills.

Rising to my feet, I feel for the round metal bulge of the door handle. Grab it. Twist. Push. The door gives.

Falling through, I spin and shut the deadlock behind me just as my hold on sound slips away. Bracing my back against the door, I survey the receiving room. A small fire burns with bright embers, smoothing the edge of the night's light chill. A small breakfast table. A settee. Several chairs. Drawn curtains. Clean. Perfect. Impersonal. A room that should belong to a palace guest, not a fourteen-year-old princess.

Moving silently through the suite, I find the door to the bedchamber and edge it open.

The light from a dying fire creeps into the royal bedroom. A girl sleeps in a large bed, the sounds of her breathing eerily familiar. I take a step forward, suddenly afraid that I'm wrong.

I'm not wrong, though. It *is* Leaf, her mouth slightly open, her hair falling onto the pillow like always. My wonderful, dear Leaf. Breath halting, I fall to my knees beside her, not caring where Violet might be. "Leaf." I shake her shoulder gently. "Leaf, wake up."

Her eyes pop open. My finger comes to my lips but I'd be unable to speak even if I wanted to. My heart races, my eyes stinging as if on fire. I swallow. She sits up like a ghost and slips her arms around me, her face buried in my shoulder.

"How?" she whispers finally. "Are you real?"

My words catch in my throat. I throw my arms around my sister and crush her to my chest. So small and frail and perfect. I repeat her name over and over, assuring myself that she is not a mirage. Assuring her that neither am I.

It's an effort to pull myself together a few heartbeats later. "Come on," I whisper. "Let's get you out of here."

She pulls away and swipes her forearm across her eyes.

Her gaze darts to the other side of the bed. "Where is Violet?" A flicker of panic. "Violet? Violet!"

I clamp a hand over Leaf's mouth. "Are you mad?"

Leaf shakes me off and slides to the floor. "We need to take Violet with us. She was here. I'm only in her bed to keep her company."

I let out a slow breath. There is no time for this. Each moment we talk puts Leaf in greater danger. "Leaf, Violet isn't a friend."

"She is confused and overwhelmed and lonely," says Leaf. "We can't just leave her. She's been through too much already."

A chill runs through my blood. Both at Leaf's innocence and my own cruel knowledge. Raza had been through a great deal as well. Right before she took a stim crystal to me and brushed her hair while my nerves frayed in agony.

I find Leaf's eyes. "We can't trust Violet. She'll betray us all. I think she may have already." My voice steadies, a calm, unwavering tone. "We need to leave. Now. Put on your shoes and follow me."

Leaf fumbles for her boots. "Who is 'us all'?" she asks quietly.

My stomach churns. I've been with friends while she suffered alone. I'd hoped to have time to explain, but we must hurry. "Prince Wil, Rune, er . . . Trace. Some others. We freed all of Bahir's whisperers. Hundreds of people he's kept enslaved in the abbey." I pause, studying her face, her eyes wide with shock, her hands covering parted lips. I swallow. "I was going to have us join them, but we don't have to, Leaf. We can go anywhere you want. I don't care where, so long as it's with you."

She pulls away from me. "What have you done?" Her eyes are wide. Terrified.

"Leaf, please," I whisper desperately. "You think I don't know that you've every reason in the world to hate me just now? I left you. I aided hundreds of others before my own sister. I don't deserve you. But please, please just come now and hate me later. We've no time."

"Don't be an idiot, Kali." Leaf grips my shoulders, aghast. Her eyes bore into mine. "The problem isn't that you did what you had to in order to survive. It's that you've just killed everyone in Dansil."

28

KALI

I run through the hidden passages toward the exit, my sword pounding against my thigh, my heart keeping beat with my steps. Leaf's words haunt my every breath. My face, drained of blood, stares without seeing. Stars. *Stars.* What have we done?

I don't see the man stepping from the shadows until his arms are around my waist, pulling me in toward him. Only his scent stays my arm from launching a dagger.

"I thought you'd turn up here sooner or later." Rune's voice drips with both reprimand and relief. He pulls me away from him long enough to place his hand over my galloping heart. "Something's happened." Not a question.

I nod anyway. It's all I can manage.

"Something so big, you are not even cursing me for almost getting myself skewered just now," says Rune.

I meet his gaze, no longer caring whether he condemns me for going after Leaf.

"I know *why* Bahir enslaves whisperers," I say, the words

tumbling from my mouth. "It's not just that he's a mage and wants no competition from them. He *needs* them. To keep the Eye of the Goddess stable. That orb, it's not just an oversized light crystal. It produces light, yes, but it does more than that. Leaf, she's done research, taken soil samples, and," I swallow, "and she touched the Eye when Bahir's guards held her in the abbey. Bahir uses his captive whisperers to keep it tuned."

Rune puts his hands on either side of my head. "What did Leaf learn?" he asks softly.

"The Eye affects Dansil's climate. Its magic is toxic. If—when—the Eye loses tune, the toxic rays will scatter like wildfire. They will kill every person in half the kingdom's radius."

Rune stiffens, his face tight as his mind comprehends the words. "The Drought?"

"Even tuned and controlled, the Eye spills some toxins in its rays. Infants are too weak to survive it." Drawing a breath, I steel myself against the passage wall, the screams of Zalia's pregnant friend, who we forced to accompany the whisperers, fresh in my memory. "There is more. Bahir has been spawning with his female followers. The pregnant mothers are warned that going aboveground will kill the child."

"The latter might be a lie to keep the girls in line," says Rune. In thought, not challenge. "Is there evidence that staying belowground protects the infants?"

"Yes. There is no Drought in the Order, Rune. Bahir houses the whisperers in the abbey, but the young children and pregnant mothers are all kept beneath the ground." I shut my eyes. "He doesn't just want to rule Dansil. He wants to be a god."

For a heartbeat, the only sounds in the passage are the quiet whispers of our breaths. Then Rune speaks, softly but without fear. "Is the Eye tuned to Bahir's blood? Were the girls mistaken when they said it was not?"

"No." I wince. "I can only draw a crystal's magic if it's tuned to my blood, but Bahir must know another way of tapping into a crystal's magic and is doing so with the Eye." I shake myself. "But that little matters now. With the whisperers gone, the Eye will become unstable shortly."

"When?" asks Rune, calculations dancing through his eyes. "Months? Weeks? Days?"

"Hours," I whisper. "Unless I stop it."

"Unless we stop it," corrects Rune.

"THIS PLAN IS LUDICROUS." Rune secures the rope around my waist and shifts the pack on his shoulders into a more comfortable position. We stand in shadow by a far temple wall. Around us, the moonlit stillness of night shatters against the uproar in the abbey behind the temple, where all the roses are now flocking, trying to close the proverbial barn gates after the horses have already run. Guards shout to each other. Voices argue the merits of going after the whisperers immediately, while the trail remains hot, or waiting until morning so there is light to see by. So long as they keep arguing there instead of patrolling here, they are welcome to debate all they like.

"You have a better one?" I slide my hand along the rough wall. The climb would be palatable if not for the small barrels of explosive powder we each carry on our backs. "Plus, I recall us saying something similar a couple weeks ago about freeing the whisperers from the abbey."

"You mean the mess we are trying to clear up now?"

Well, there is that.

"I suppose we could go inside instead and ask one of the holy guardsmen to show us to the roof."

Rune growls. "Hilarious."

"I know." I test the rope, a curtain of shadow secure around Rune and me. My reserve of magic is nearly drained, but once we are on the roof, there should be little need for darkness. I step up to the wall and find my first foothold. Standing on the ground, Rune feeds the rope out as I climb the first few paces and anchor in. With a tug, I signal my success to Rune and climb on by feel only until I find the next attractive point to drive in an anchor spike. Secure the second anchor. Signal. Climb again. When the rope reaches its full length, my shadow stretching below me to cover us both, I find solid footing and take in the line while Rune climbs up to my ledge.

Then we do it again, brushing our fingers along each other's flesh in reassurance each time we pass within reach.

My arms tremble by the time we scale the temple's sloping roof toward the flat platform at its zenith. I release my hold on the shadow. The wind, as if offended at the intrusion, picks up with a howl. My hair whips across my cheeks. Grasping the platform's edge, I haul myself onto it, only to jerk back when the Eye's brightness hits me with the force of a physical blow.

My sweaty hand springs reflexively to my eyes, my precarious hold wobbling. Rune's hand presses solidly into the small of my back. My balance steadies. Tapping deeper into my precious well of magic, I deflect the Eye's light until it no longer threatens to burn our eyes.

"Thank the stars," Rune breathes. His hand leaves my back, though I still feel the ghost of his touch lingering on my skin. With battlefield efficiency, Rune unties the rope from his waist and secures the line to a stone gargoyle at the eastern corner of the roof.

I start to ease my pack off my shoulders and feel Rune behind me, taking its weight. We repeat the same trick with

Rune's pack. Neither of us dares breathe until the barrels of powder stand solid on the roof floor.

Turning my back to the pedestal holding the Eye, I survey the city sprawling beneath us. Small houses. Shops. The occasional night worker scurrying along empty streets. Delta going about its life, oblivious to the death looming over it.

"Are you certain about this?" Rune asks. "You are permitted to change your mind, if your gut tells you to."

I swallow. "I'm certain."

His gray gaze skips up to mine, his silvery hair whipping around his angled face in the wind. He squints in the Eye's fluctuating light despite my efforts to shield us from it. "And I'm certain in you."

Warmth rises in my chest and I press my lips against his, indulging in a moment of stolen pleasure before yanking myself back.

Focus on the bloody barrels of black powder. The Eye flashes, the light striking deep into my eyes despite my deflection. Stars dance in my vision, a headache cutting through my brain. I realize I've stopped moving only when Rune calls my name. Rain has joined the rising wind, and I blink both away.

"The pack's cloth is too thin, and the barrels aren't watertight," Rune says, positioning himself to shield the fuse and powder from the rain. He shouts to be heard over the wind's howl. "They won't keep the powder dry enough to work. Can you deflect the rain the way you do light and sound?"

Right. "I love trying new things in the middle of a bloody storm with explosives in my hands," I murmur. But Rune is right. I reach into my magic reserves and beg the stars to make deflecting water easier than absorbing sound.

It isn't. It feels like pushing back a river with my bare

hands. For each particle of the streaking water that I manage to capture and deflect, a hundred more stream by like arrows.

"It's not working," Rune informs me, his voice so calm I want to kick him. "Try something else." Another gust of cold, wet wind.

My barrel of powder shudders. I grab for it, miss, and watch the fuse topple to the stone. A scream builds in my lungs, stopping in my throat as the fuse rolls back and forth like a child's toy on the roof. I snatch it up. The terror of certain death ebbs, but the stupidity of this whole plan hits me full force. I know nothing of explosives, and I'm trying to save a kingdom by blowing a living crystal the size of three men into pieces when I can't even keep control of the fuse.

"It's all right, Kali," says Rune. Calm. Steady. Strong. A bloody excellent liar. "You are all right."

I draw in a shaking breath. I have to shield the powder against wind and rain. Have to. If I don't, I fail Leaf and all the people in Dansil whose lives I so carelessly toyed with. My chest clenches into a painful knot.

I plunge into my magic and throw it with abandon at the elements. No portioning, no reserves. Just the rawness of whatever power I have within me against the wind and the rain and the world.

The world laughs.

It might have worked had I any magic left in my well. My throat closes with a sob.

"Enough!" Rune's order battles the wind. He grabs the barrels of black powder and the fuse from my hand and covers them with his body. "We set the fuse as is. Let's move."

Even that proves more difficult than I expected. The light of the Eye increases exponentially with each step. Rune hisses in pain, covering his eyes with a forearm.

I scrape my magic dry, forcing every bit of my life force

into the effort to keep the Eye's light from scorching us blind. My limbs feel like they're swimming through sand. I focus on words, hold on to them like a rope as we prepare to set our charge. "How . . . do you think . . . whisperers get close . . . enough to tune this?"

"They work from beneath the roof."

It takes me a heartbeat to realize the answering voice is not Rune's, but Bahir's.

29

KALI

*M*y body reacts before I do, slipping a knife free into my palm.

Bahir steps out from behind the Eye, his voice clear and booming. "It takes a special kind of imbecile to climb atop this roof." The bishop pats the glowing orb and rests his palm on its belly, as if soothing a beloved pet. A band of dark, intricate glass covers his eyes. His red robes and black hair billow in the wind. He wags a finger at me, his heavy ring shimmering like a mirror. The same ring that sent a shock of pain through me at King Firehorn's dinner party. "You've angered the Goddess now. Her gift is not so tame anymore."

I throw my knife into Bahir's chest. It slams against an invisible wall and skids harmlessly to the floor.

With a flick of his boot, Bahir kicks my dagger off the edge. "I wonder whether you can do better than that, little mage. And whether you are worth breaking to bridle."

Rune shifts his weight in a way I know too well, his fingers tightening around the hilt of his sword.

"Don't," I yell at him, my eyes on the black powder he hugs to his body.

"She's right, princeling," Bahir croons. "Some of that powder is still dry enough. Jar the keg around and it *will* spark. Your entrails will rain down on Delta before you get close enough to nick me with your toy."

Rune grinds his jaw. "We know the Eye is unstable without the whisperers," he says, his voice too reasonable for the madness around us. Time. He is giving me time. I slide carefully sideways toward Bahir's blind spot. Rune tilts his blade, catching the light on its gleaming surface. "You must know it too, Bahir. You must want control of Dansil's people, not their corpses."

"I want nothing," Bahir snaps. "I am but a vessel of the Goddess's will."

I slide another inch. Then another.

"My mistake," says Rune, "but wouldn't your Goddess, too, prefer her disciples alive?"

Another shift of weight. I'm three paces from Bahir's free hand. I slip another dagger into my palm. Another few heartbeats and, if Bahir keeps his head still, I'll slip past the edge of his vision.

"Bahir!" Rune's voice booms as if shouting across a field of battle. "Help us save your Goddess's people!"

"I think you've *helped* quite enough." Bahir throws his hand out toward me. A spear of flame materializes at my throat, its tip scorching my skin.

I freeze.

"Set the powder down, boy," Bahir instructs Rune. "And uncover it."

"No!" I yell. Rune's eyes lock on my throat and the crisp burn spreading across my skin. "No," I say again.

But he tightens his jaw and obeys Bahir's command. "Let her go," he demands.

"Now, remove the fuse," says Bahir. When Rune hesitates, the glowing spear at my throat traces the line of my jaw.

I stiffen against the pain, the stench of burned flesh filling my nostrils. Rune removes the fuse, which falls away harmlessly from the quickly soaking powder. My heart sinks.

Rune turns his face to Bahir. "Let her go."

"I've not yet determined her to be a lost cause," Bahir purrs.

Rune's face darkens. He steps toward Bahir, his chest out. "You need the whisperers back to stabilize the Eye. Kalianna plotted their course. Send her to fetch them and keep me as collateral."

My eyes widen, my face snapping to Rune's. "Have you lost your mind?"

"Children!" Bahir holds up his hand, the spear at my throat not wavering a hair. "No need for squabbles. I believe my men are bright enough to follow ribbons without your expertise." Reaching into his pocket, Bahir pulls out one of my markers.

My breath catches, my lungs unable to fill themselves as I stare at the bit of cloth in his fingers.

"Come out, my lady," Bahir calls, holding out his ringed hand.

Violet steps out from behind the Eye. Taking the offered hand, she kisses the ring before intertwining her small fingers with his. The dark band around her eyes, a sibling to Bahir's, hides little of her face. "I admit I little believed Princess Raza at first." Violet tilts her head, studying Rune's pale face. "It was such an unlikely story. But when I learned there was an attack on the abbey, it seemed wise to seek the Messenger's guidance."

I shake my head, no words coming to my tongue.

"Renounce the Dark God," Violet's young voice rings through the air. "Accept the Goddess into your heart, Lady Kalianna. Cleanse yourself of your sins, Prince Rune. Choose to live. Choose to save your soul."

"Open your eyes, Violet," I hiss. "The Order kills people. Ask your Messenger about the Drought."

The spear at my throat dips to brand my collarbone, and I howl.

Violet's hand tightens in Bahir's. "It's a necessary price for our fertile fields and kind weather. Those who've accepted the Goddess into their hearts and borne their children beneath the Order's sanctuary suffer no ill effects. Only those who refuse to hear the Messenger's word suffer the Goddess's wrath."

I grind my teeth. "Violet, your father—"

"Stop." She thrusts her free palm toward me. "Listen to me. You are still alive because the Messenger believes your soul not yet lost to the Dark God. The battle between the Dark God's evil and the Goddess's love is waging within you this very moment. Choose the side of love, Kalianna. Swear your allegiance to the Goddess and let the Messenger guide and train you to serve her will."

I stare at Violet's eyes beyond the darkened glass of her visor. Large, determined, lashes as long as Wil's. My friend's little sister. My cousin. The girl who betrayed us all.

Violet's lips move, though no words come from her mouth. *Kali. Kali. Kali.*

My brows twitch.

No! Don't move. Leaf said you can read lips. Violet takes a sharp breath. Her free hand curls around her skirt in a white-knuckle grip. Despite the wind and rain, her skin looks flushed. My heart slams against my ribs. I stay frozen except for a small, nervous glance at Rune and Bahir. Uncertain. Considering. It's all I can do to buy Violet a few moments to find her words. Whether those words can be trusted is another matter.

I've been watching. I think Bahir's ring is his key, Violet's lips say silently. *Maybe it can be yours.* The next moment, Violet turns her hand in Bahir's grip, grabs the ring, and yanks it off his finger.

The spear of flame at my throat falters. Violet goes to throw the ring but crumples to the ground mid-step, her body convulsing.

I sprint toward her as Rune rushes Bahir, the prince's sword raised high. The moment my skin touches the ring clutched in Violet's spasming fingers, bees shoot out across my skin. The ring must be akin to a stim crystal—one that's stopping Violet's heart.

The agony in the girl's eyes spills over us. The bones of her small fingers threaten to break under my attempts to pry open her fist and remove the ring from its grip.

I force my breathing to slow, bracing myself for the influx of the ring's magic. It comes, but not in the way I expect. Magic siphons into my body, coating my nerves like oil, and stops. No replenishment of my reserves, no diversion from Violet's assault.

Whatever in the rutting hells this ring is, it's unlike anything I've felt before.

Violet's lips darken from lack of blood and air. I scrape my palm open on the rough stone, but even the direct contact with my blood changes nothing. Clenching my teeth, I ignore the crack of bone as I force the ring from Violet's grip. I slide it onto my finger at the same moment as Bahir bellows my name.

I jerk my head up.

For the first time since stepping foot on the roof, Bahir is away from the Eye. He stands now with one arm pointed at Rune, who's standing too close to the platform's edge.

Rune bends against an unnatural concoction of wind and rain that drives him backward toward death.

"The Goddess's sacred gift is not for you, Kalianna," Bahir roars at me, his wind forcing Rune back another step. Then another. "Return it now or the boy's life is forfeit."

Panic washes over me. A barrel of black powder topples onto its side, taking the other one down with it. I watch them roll off the roof as if in slow motion. What dry powder remained in their bellies sparks at the collision with the cobblestones below. The boom of the small explosion echoes through the streets. Our one means of breaking apart the Eye, gone in a flash.

"The ring, girl!" Bahir turns his palm up. "Throw it to me."

"No!" Rune shouts.

My mouth dries. I raise the hand with the ring to my face, staring between the artifact and the bishop. Despite wearing the ring, my reserves remain empty. Perhaps Violet was wrong when she thought the ring valuable enough to risk her life for. Or maybe the ring and I are simply incompatible. Perhaps that oily sheen that covers my innards is the final mark of my failure.

Perhaps the ring is useless to me. Rune is not.

"Don't do it," Rune yells. His sword is gone. His arms try and fail to stave off Bahir's assault. Silver hair, damp with rain, whips in Rune's face. "Don't give him anything."

Bahir wheels on Rune. With the next heartbeat, Rune loses his footing. His body skids toward the edge of the platform, fingers grasping for purchase. His head strikes the gargoyle, and his body goes slack for a moment before toppling over.

The world ends. I scream, falling to my knees.

30

KALI

*E*ven Bahir stands frozen for an instant. Then he turns toward me slowly and smiles, showing his teeth. The wind settles. "You made me do that. No one else. You."

A sob chokes me.

Bahir's voice changes, taking a fatherly tone. Slow and rhythmic. "Come, child. It is time to end this madness before you cause more needless suffering and death."

My heart squeezes.

"You think I don't know you, Lady Kalianna?" says Bahir, taking a step toward me, the heels of his boots clicking against the roof. "I do. Your father never wanted you. Your mother died. Your master sent you away. Your king used you." He snaps his tongue, shaking his head mournfully. Another step. Another click of his boots. "It's little wonder that after all that, you followed their example. You abandoned your gender. Left a city of innocents in the midst of bloodshed. Why, in just the past quarter hour, you killed a young girl and a valiant prince. Perhaps you stand alone now because you deserve to be." His brows pull together, his palms opening before him. "The Goddess is laying the truth bare before you. You can't deny it. You feel it in your blood, don't you?"

I shake my head. Bahir can't know whether Violet is dead. My vision blurs as I watch her small, still form. No movement. No breath.

"You killed them," Bahir repeats, softer now. Like a lullaby. *Click. Click. Click.*

No. No, *I* didn't kill them . . . Except . . . except that it is my fault. Mine and my schemes'.

"There is no one left, girl," Bahir whispers, his steps stilling. "No one but me and the Goddess. So pull yourself together and listen. You know nothing of your true capabilities. Can you do this?" The spear of flame appears next to him again, but stays hovering in the air like an obedient dog. "Can you shield yourself from it?"

I can barely breathe. I want the spear to pierce my heart. Salt melts in my mouth.

Bahir's voice rises again, his hands extending toward me. "I can teach you. Think of the good you can do once you harness the Goddess's gift."

My eyes sting. I don't want the Goddess's gift. I want Rune. As badly as Bahir wants the ring. Stars, I should have traded one for the other. I would have. For better or for worse, I know in my heart that I would have.

And Rune, Rune who's been able to read my face since I first came to Delta, he knew it too—knew it before I did and let himself die to prevent me from making that choice.

A chill runs over me. I rise to my feet. My soulmate— because that's what he was—gave his life for my fight. This night, I will make his sacrifice count. Whether the ring condescends to tell me its secrets or not.

Bahir's smile falters. His robes whip majestically behind

him, their yellow accents the color of the glowing spear. I stare at the magical weapon, which is still hovering instead of taking up its former post at my throat. Why? Why the talk, the moving around? Even if Bahir seeks not my death but my obedience, why not bind and shackle me now?

My hands curl around the ring on my finger. I watch Bahir's face, extracting information from his body the way I've been trained to.

His gaze is strained, creasing his forehead. His shoulders, though hidden beneath heavy fabric, hunch. A bead of sweat trickles down his temple, dissolving into his goatee. Yes, Bahir is straining, just as I am. He's preserving his strength and his magic, afraid to waste a drop.

Yet he was unafraid before. Felt no need to preserve his magic. Not until . . . not until Violet. As if when Violet removed his ring, she cut off his supply line. And gave it to me. Except the bloody thing isn't working.

Or . . .

My eyes narrow. When Bahir first appeared, I watched him stroke the Eye like a pet. But he isn't stroking it now, is he? Why? Why did Bahir hold on to the Eye while wearing the ring, and why stay away from it now? A living crystal isn't a mage's pet; it's his power source. *If* said mage has the conduit necessary to siphon the crystal's magic.

The final piece of the puzzle snaps into place and I dive for the Eye.

Bahir hurls a ball of flame at me, no longer bothering to forge the magic into a weapon's shape.

I roll over my shoulder to avoid the projectile, which slams into the Eye behind me. The Eye shudders and icy thunder rolls through the sky. Rising to my feet, I press my hand flush against the Eye of the Goddess. The ring on my finger pulsates in time with my heart.

The stinging bees are a mere echo of the awesome force within the Eye. Magic sears through me, only that oily coating of the ring protecting my nerves from exploding into dust. The ring pulses harder, mirroring my heart, harmonizing my body with the Eye's power. Tapping the living crystal's magic.

Magic. Magic. Magic. It roars inside me. A wild, dangerous animal on the verge of tearing me to pieces.

I realize I've forgotten to breathe and force in a lungful of air. It surges in, ice cold and cutting. The wind that blew rain into my face now blows snow.

"Stop, idiot girl," Bahir hollers. He stands on one knee, bending against the storm, robe streaming like a banner behind him. "You know nothing of what you touch. The Eye of the Goddess protects Dansil." His voice echoes in the thunder.

My heart pounds.

"You will kill them all," Bahir yells. "The children. The innocents. The whole kingdom will be laid to ruin at your feet." He throws both arms toward me, a deadly spray of magical shrapnel exploding from his fingertips. Shards of blood-red fire and orange light, of gray wind and blue ice. Magic grand and bright enough to light the whole sky and eclipse the stars for its flash of power.

I throw out a wall of pure magic and the shrapnel recoils, stray shards of flame and ice piercing Bahir's body, the bits of wind lifting him off his feet. Bahir screams, his feet flailing and never finding purchase before the magic that he himself cast knocks him off the temple roof.

My shield shatters, my well of magic draining in the blink of an eye and refilling again from the living crystal. The wind dies and rises. The Eye flashes. So unstable. So dangerous. So powerful. My lungs burn. I've forgotten to breathe again. My vision blurs, clears. My heart beats in the rhythm of the Eye. Erratic. Burning hot. Ice cold.

I long for shadow. The Eye's light dims.

"Kali!" The voice calling my name is both familiar and displaced. Rune's. Calling from the underworld. Or from the stars. I've forgotten whether I'm inhaling or exhaling. "Kali!" Rune calls again. From below. Not the stars, then.

Hands grab the gargoyle and a lithe body pulls itself up onto the roof. Silver-blond hair, emerald-tinged gray eyes shining in the Eye's orange light. It can't be.

Rune releases the rope. It swings back down from the gargoyle's neck. Bending against the wind, he starts toward me. "Where is Bahir?" he hollers over the storm.

I can't answer. I don't know. And I don't know how to say that I don't know.

Cursing, Rune fights his way over to me. "Kali, look at me."

I do. My chest hurts. The relief of seeing Rune is making my knees buckle, but I cannot even tell him that. Can't say anything.

Rune yanks the healing stone from his neck and wraps its cord quickly around his fingers. Drawing the knife from his boot, he opens a shallow cut along his palm, then another across mine. Our hands connect, the living stone pressed between our bloodied palms. Rune's face goes taut, but a moment later, my chest expands with breath. Again. Again. Steady and smooth. My eyes regain their focus.

"Are you breathing for me?" I try to ask. The words sound muffled, my tongue too big for my mouth.

"Yes," says Rune. "Since you can't be bothered to do it yourself."

I blink. Another breath comes into my lungs. In and out. It

feels good. The Eye pulsates. I can't be both with the Eye and with myself. I've not the skill Bahir had.

"Do it, Kali," Rune says softly, studying my face. Reading my thoughts. "Destroy the Eye."

"Can't," I croak.

"Yes, you can," says Rune through clenched teeth. "You are a warrior and you can. You will." His eyes find mine, stare into my soul. "And while you do, I will breathe for you. I will pace your heart. Trust me to keep you alive while you do the same for the rest of us. Trust me, Kali. Please."

I do. Abandoning my body to Rune's control, I focus all my being on the Eye's magic. I drink all that I can, and more, so much more. And then, like bending light to create shadow, I reflect all the magic back into the living crystal.

Until it cracks.

KALI

J wake to a soft feather mattress hugging my body. Snow, white as my sheets, sparkles beyond a velvet-curtained window. Everything hurts. I shift my head to the side and have the disorienting feeling of being both alert and asleep, as if one of my limbs failed to awaken with the rest of me. I check and find all my limbs accounted for.

"There you are." A disheveled Wil springs up from the chair beside my bed. "Rune will be pissed as a hungry bear. He's been waiting for you to wake up for three days." Wil grins.

Rune. That's the sleeping limb. I'm not sure how I know it, but I do. Just as I know that he's waking up now and that Wil's prediction is right.

"What happened?" I ask.

Wil sprawls back into his chair and swings one leg over the side. "Let's see . . . A few hundred whisperers and I were all wondering where in the bloody hells you and Rune had disappeared to, when the Eye of the Goddess exploded into shards and the weather turned to Everett."

I lick dry lips, the memories returning slowly. The rooftop, the Eye. "Bahir?"

Wil hands me a glass of water. When he thinks I'm not paying attention, a lake of worry and fatigue fills his eyes. "Luca's men have been going through the temple rubble. They don't think they've found him yet." With visible effort, Wil chases the shadow from his face. "But it's hard to identify the bodies. We may have him buried already and not know it."

I swallow. "Of course. There is nowhere else for him to have gone." A lie. But perhaps it's all right to lie to yourself sometimes. Even if Bahir is still alive, he's castrated without his ring and Eye and whisperers. At least for now.

"We did find Bahir's journals in his room," Wil adds. "I think Leaf is in her own personal paradise amidst the pages. It appears that Bahir has been working toward seizing control of Dansil for decades, ever since discovering himself a mage and starting to hoard living crystals for their power. Everett seizing control of the Sylthia mines shattered a lot of his plans. He'd gotten the Eye out of Sylthia before the attack, but was never able to return for other large pieces. It drove him mad with fury. Especially once Everett started breaking down large stones into small, practical chunks for transport and sale."

"Was the Drought always part of his plan?" I ask.

"Not originally. Bahir intended to harness the Eye's magic into a weapon, but it didn't work out. Something about the breed of the crystal not being what he needed. So he changed tactics, decided to make the most of what he did have until he could get Sylthia back." Wil shrugs. "Bahir called the Eye's effects 'unexpected but fortunate and illuminating.' I think he really believed himself to be the Goddess's chosen."

Yes, he probably did. "And the ring?" I frown at my empty

hand. "It allowed Bahir—and me—to siphon the Eye's magic directly."

"Melted into goo when the Eye shattered. Leaf is trying to figure out where he might have gotten it, but as of now, you are back to siphoning the old way." Wil sighs. "After seizing Dansil, Bahir planned on retaking Sylthia and harvesting more stones to feed his power. The whisperers he collected were being groomed to tune and stabilize whatever other crystals Bahir obtained. The man was nothing if not thorough."

I rub my eyes. "Leaf. Where is she?"

Wil reclaims his smile. "Supervising the relocation of the Eye's debris beneath the ground. She says it's safest for now, until the pieces can be examined for . . ." He runs his hands through his hair. "I don't know for what, actually. She so bored me with her explanations that I just put her in charge of it all. I can do such things now. Even more so once I am crowned king. Not bad, right?"

My heart squeezes, the one name not yet mentioned stoking my fears. "Violet, is she . . ." I choke back the words as the frightening truth shows in Wil's eyes. My next words come as a whisper. "She destroyed herself when she got Bahir's ring for me, didn't she?"

"No." Wil pulls back, life leeching from his voice. "She destroyed herself when she realized she'd handed our father's head and throne to a monster. She was already a shell when she stepped onto that roof. She just wanted to do something right before leaving."

No. *No, no, no.* I snatch his hand. "Violet drew Bahir to that roof to discover the conduit he used to harness the Eye's power. She went up there to fight. She was a hero."

He shakes his head and touches his breast pocket, a piece of paper crinkling beneath his fingers. A letter. "Violet took her life before she ever set foot on that roof. Drank a poison that Leaf kept amidst her medicines. She . . ." Wil's eyes glisten and he turns his face away. "She said she wanted her death to matter since her life hadn't." My breath catches, no words coming to my rescue. Wil swallows. "I miss the little fool," he whispers, squeezing my hand once and then straightening. A prince. A ruler. "I think I hear footsteps."

I frown as much from the shift in topic as from the realization that the steps Wil was just hearing, I've been feeling for some time. Rune is coming. The door bursts open to let in a bare-chested silver-haired storm that launches an apple at my sheet-covered torso.

"I'm gone," Wil says, saluting and scampering out the door.

"Coward!" I call after him.

Rune growls and points at the apple. "Eat. You're hungry."

I rub the back of my head. "No, I'm not. I think that may be you."

He snatches the apple from me and bites into it. "Bloody brilliant."

"Rune," I say softly.

Lowering the apple, Rune hoists himself onto the bed beside me and extends his hand to my face, gently cupping my chin.

I press into him like a cat, my skin warming in response.

Rune's hands slide down my body, tracing my shoulders, brushing the swell of my chest, and—

Need and desire, mine and not mine, pulse through my core so hard that my breath catches. "Stars." I draw breath, looking at Rune, at the hard bulge in his breeches and, finally, his flaming red face. "Oh, bloody stars."

He winces. "Yes, there is that. Not that you shouldn't know that I want you, it's just . . . I'd rather be able to tell you that myself than let this . . . whatever it is . . . do it for me."

"I don't understand."

Rune pulls away with visible effort. "Your heart, your breath, they were all mine after the Eye shattered. I was so afraid to sleep for fear of taking your air. It's gotten better. No one knows whether we'll ever be truly . . . separate again."

"I don't care." The truth of the words grips my heart. "I don't want to be."

Rune's mouth lowers to cover mine, and where I end and he begins is suddenly a moot point.

THE BALCONY OVERLOOKING the palace courtyard is cold, flakes of gentle snow swaying down from a clear sky. People crowding the yard below pull their cloaks tight and tentatively take the small heat crystals that children offer in baskets. Having the children bring around tuned crystals was Raza's idea. And it's working.

The princess's gaze follows her charges' progress. Satisfied, she steps back into the shadows and pulls her hood further over her head.

Striding up to where Wil, Rune, and I stand behind the balcony's side curtains, Calvin bows formally. "It's time."

My heart pounds, my palms sweating despite the cold. "I'll wait for you here," I whisper desperately. "I'm a scout. I don't do crowds."

"I understand," says Wil in a voice so empathetic, it sets the hair at the nape of my neck on end. The next heartbeat, Rune drops a chip of ice down the back of my dress.

I gasp.

Grinning, Rune and Wil each grab an elbow and march me out to the center of the balcony between them.

"I'm going to murder you in your sleep," I tell Wil. He has the decency to pale before taking a step forward to the railing.

"His Royal Majesty William Firehorn, King of Dansil!" announces the herald.

The crowd cheers. Rune squeezes my hand.

Snow dancing around his long lashes, Wil raises his head high. "People of Dansil!" he calls. Picking up the strands of his voice with my magic, I project the sound over the courtyard. "It's our first winter in two decades, and I'll endeavor to stop speaking before we all turn to ice. Today we welcome an Everett ambassador as a resident of the Delta Royal Palace. Dansil welcomes you, Prince Rune, especially your expertise on warm clothes and warmer fires."

A small chuckle brushes the crowd. I start smiling too until—

"We also celebrate Lady Kalianna, my cousin and a mage, who has brought an end to the Drought in our lands."

"What?" The word is out of my mouth before I realize I'm speaking. And projecting. The courtyard's chuckling morphs into full-bellied laughter. My teeth grind. "Wil, you are so dead," I promise, remembering this time to keep the words from echoing in the winds. Then, little caring whether Wil just introduced me or not, I back slowly from the balcony.

And find Rune's solidness blocking my way. "Going somewhere?" he whispers into my ear. I dig my nails into the soft flesh between his thumb and forefinger. "Curtsy to them," he murmurs. "They *want* to celebrate you."

Seeing that there is no help for it, I dip to the floor, my face heating as the attention of many faces brushes and pokes and tickles my skin. I take a breath and drink it all in, the energy and excitement resonating against my chest. And then I do something I never expected—I rise and smile. No, I grin. I *wave.* I share my joy and accept theirs in return.

The crowd breaks into applause that rings in my ears long after everyone has dispersed and I'm curled up in an armchair in Wil's sitting room. The others file in one by one, finding their own favorite seats. Wil and Leaf, Rune and Raza, Luca and Calvin. I take out a dagger and twirl it in my hand.

"You can't still be mad," says Wil, throwing a pillow to the floor and sprawling atop it like a disheveled hound. "I know you enjoyed it. Eventually. Rune told me."

I scowl at him. "You two could have told me you were planning to thrust me in front of the whole bloody city like a prize peacock."

"If we had, I'd have had to carry you bodily onto that balcony." Rune pours wine into goblets, the sweet, fruity smell filling the air. "Not that I would've minded, but it might have sent the wrong message about this new peace and cooperation and all that. And we need my father's spies to deliver the proper wording. He'll be delighted to learn of this new alliance, I'm certain."

Wil and I snort together.

"Speaking of spies, I've written to Lord Gapral," I tell Wil. "He won't travel to Delta—it's a matter of professional principle to keep his face from being seen more than it must— but he's happy to continue supporting the throne. I can stop by the estate in six months or so for a better sense of strategy."

"Excellent. Always a pleasure when someone volunteers to be the palace's resident spymaster," says Wil.

I snap bolt upright in my seat. "That's not what I said, Wil."

He grins. "Sure it is. And you are hereby appointed."

"I'll kill you," I growl.

"Before the king is murdered, might we address one other matter with Everett?" Raza's voice interrupts tentatively from the corner of the room. She passes a letter to Wil. "Might you see that my father gets this?"

"What is it?" asks Wil.

Raza adjusts her hood. "The details of my death. He'll accept it. Everett has an heir again. Or will once the news of today's announcement reaches the Everett palace."

Rune takes the letter from Wil and chucks it into the fire. "No more."

"I can be something here, Rune," says Raza with no hint of submission. "The former *Children*, the freed whisperers, the girls and their babies and shattered families, everyone whose life just got stripped of the only meaning they thought it had— who is going to take charge of them? Who will make certain they don't just relive their history? Are you? Is *she*?"

"At least I've graduated from 'whore' to 'she,'" I mumble. Raza and I will never be friends, but the passing days do seem to nudge us from I'd-like-to-kill-you-in-horrid-ways to mere potent hatred.

"What Raza needs is a title," says Wil, gesturing with a half-eaten apple that he pulled from stars-know-where. He and Luca are kindred souls when it comes to their stomachs.

"She *has* a title," says Rune.

"Princess isn't a title. Not the kind that matters." Wil's gaze looks at something beyond the walls, his fingers touching a familiar spot on his breast pocket. "Not the kind that helps you find a place."

Leaf reaches out and gently brushes Wil's hand. The young king gives her a tight smile. Tight and brotherly. I smile. Luca, pristine in his uniform and now captain of the guard, catches my eye and nods at the unspoken thought. Yes, we are all melding together. A family of our own making.

"How about Minister of Integration?" says Calvin, checking the steeping tea. Satisfied, he fills the cups and offers the first two to Wil and Leaf, who instantly disappear into the soothing brew. "Raza is correct that the Order's collapse left a great many young people with shattered worlds. Let us not lose more of them than we must."

Wil nods without looking up. "I'm unsure what we've in the budget, but—"

"Wil, the day you know what's in a budget is the day Kali becomes a dressmaker," Leaf says with a roll of her eyes. She turns to Raza. "Delta's abandoned Whisperer Guild headquarters has dormitories. Enough for temporary housing while things are sorted. We can stock supplies and get it ready for occupancy quickly enough."

"Why would I need to know what's in a budget when you can bloody memorize anything you see and spit it back on command?" Wil says to Leaf before he, too, turns to Raza. "Clearly, my brilliance lies in surrounding myself with the right people. What do you think, Minister?"

"I think," Raza says softly. "I think that I'll call it Violet Abbey."

EPILOGUE

Standing on a rooftop above the Wandering Dog's alley, I press deep into the shadows. A man's footsteps approach. I only hear them because he wants me to, and I shuffle my own feet to confirm my presence—the days of Rune and me just *knowing* each other's precise location passed moons ago. The connection remaining between us limits itself to sharing emotional peaks and general whereabouts.

No doubt, Rune is here now because he felt my thrill and grew curious. Or needlessly worried.

"Is there a reason you're playing with rats today?" he asks, his low voice a caress against my ear. "Or do you simply enjoy driving me out of my mind? Did you know I was in the middle of greeting Everett's newest envoy when enough excitement to send a pig squealing rushed through my veins?"

"You actually squealed?"

"I said—" Rune cuts off with a small growl as he catches the humor on my face.

I lay my hand on his cheek, the light prickle of his skin warm beneath my cold palm. His heart beats a harmony to my own, each stroke echoing through my body. The strength and power that is Rune encircles me like a blanket. The practical side of me little needs Rune here to help me hunt, but the rest of me sings at his presence.

Rune's lips brush my ear. "If driving me mad was indeed your end goal, I must congratulate you for achieving it."

My breath quickens. Stars. I force myself to stare at a real rat—currently scurrying across a discarded crate—just to calm my treacherous body. "I've other goals too," I murmur. "Such as weeding out Viva Sylthia parasites. Five founding members of the regrouping Delta cell went into the Wandering Dog an hour ago. They will be greeting a jail cell come morning."

Rune's sigh is one of long sufferance. "You know this isn't your job anymore."

"And you know we've no one better. Plus, it's hardly fair to let Luca's soldiers have all the fun."

A low chuckle, more of a rumble than a noise, vibrates Rune's wide chest. For all his words, I can feel the predator in Rune salivating to join in the hunt. To my ongoing surprise, where I've always preferred solitude, I welcome his company.

"Five bastards, you say?" He squeezes my hand before sliding his own to his sword. "Whichever of us has fewer wrapped up by the end of the evening has to go to *all* the diplomatic council meetings for the next week."

"That is absurdly unfair. I'm the one who found them. Making up rules to suit your own strengths is a dirty turn."

Despite the night's darkness, I swear I see Rune's eyes gleam with wicked delight. "I'll make it up to you later."

An exhilarating shiver races through my body. Before I can say more, however, the Wandering Dog's door opens and the five marks stroll onto the street.

Rune and I dissolve into the shared hunt.

Reviews are an author's lifeblood. Please consider saying a few words about this book on Amazon.

ABOUT THE AUTHOR

Alex Lidell is the Amazon Breakout Novel Awards finalist author of THE CADET OF TILDOR (Penguin, 2013). She is an avid horseback rider, a (bad) hockey player, and an ice-cream addict. Born in Russia, Alex learned English in elementary school, where a thoughtful librarian placed a copy of Tamora Pierce's ALANNA in Alex's hands. In addition to becoming the first English book Alex read for fun, ALANNA started Alex's life long love for fantasy books. Alex lives in Washington, DC. Join Alex's newsletter for news, bonus content and sneak peeks: www.subscribepage.com/TIDES Find out more on Alex's website: www.alexlidell.com

SIGN UP FOR NEWS AND RELEASE NOTIFICATIONS

Connect with Alex!
www.alexlidell.com
alex@alexlidell.com

www.ingramcontent.com/pod-product-compliance
Lightning Source LLC
Chambersburg PA
CBHW031245120726
47905CB00002B/727

9 780999 876045 2